Pascal Garnier

Pascal Garnier was born in Paris in 1949. The prize-winning author of more than sixty books, he remains a leading figure in contemporary French literature, in the tradition of Georges Simenon. He died in 2010.

Emily Boyce

Emily Boyce is in-house translator at Gallic Books. She lives in London. She has previously translated *Moon in a Dead Eye*.

D0924017

Also by Pascal Garnier:

*The Panda Theory*
*How's the Pain?*
*The A26*
*Moon in a Dead Eye*
*The Front Seat Passenger*

# The Islanders

Pascal Garnier

Translated from the French by Emily Boyce

Gallic Books

London

A Gallic Book

Original title : *Les Insulaires* © Zulma, 2010

English translation copyright © Gallic Books 2014

First published in Great Britain in 2014 by Gallic Books, 59 Ebury Street, London,
SW1W 0NZ

A CIP record for this book is available from the British Library
ISBN 978-1-908313-72-0

Typeset in Fournier MT by Gallic Books
Printed in the UK by CPI (CR0 4YY)
2 4 6 8 10 9 7 5 3 1

*There is an urgent need to create new islands.*

Alexandre Vialatte

He opened one eye. In the seat opposite, a woman in her forties was smiling to herself as she looked through a set of photos she had probably just collected. They showed a baby with vermilion-red eyes being held under the arms like a hideous chrysalis. Next to her, a rough-looking skinhead was flicking through a copy of *Sécuri-mag*, 'the number one magazine for security professionals'. He gave the impression he took his job seriously.

Olivier glanced at his watch. In three-quarters of an hour he would be in Paris. Outside was empty space which the snow, despite falling heavily, could not fill. As the train entered a tunnel, he noticed a heart traced on the steamed-up window. He wondered which of them had drawn it: the lady with the photos or the skinhead. The skinhead, without a doubt. Olivier pulled his coat up round his ears. Even on the TGV it was cold, the icy air seeping in through the tiniest crack like a toxic gas. He lowered his eyelids and tried to return to his dream. All that was left of it was odd snippets, fragments that melted like snowflakes the moment he tried to grasp them. The roof of the clinic . . .

The roof of the rehab clinic in Tain was strewn with hip flasks filled with bad rum, whisky and brandy. Theoretically, people were supposed to leave cured. Theoretically. For most patients, it was simply a warm place to spend the winter. They hardly ever got to see a doctor, but there was a ping-pong table in the common room. They knocked the ball listlessly back and forth between doses of medication.

This was the first time in two years he had thought about his detox treatment. It had not been too painful. Just boring, like military service. When he was let out two weeks later and met Odile, she asked him how he had got through it.

'I told myself that if I was on a desert island, I'd have had no choice but to give up.'

'And how do you feel now?'

'Like I'm on a desert island.'

He had married Odile.

Distracted by memories, he could not go back to his dream. A girl tottered down the aisle. Nice bum, nice shaved head, as if she knew she was pretty enough to get away with making herself ugly.

Olivier weighed up whether to take a taxi or the metro from Gare de Lyon to Gare Saint-Lazare. A taxi would be more comfortable but he had not been on the metro for a long time. He had not done many things for a long time . . . After getting out of rehab he had decided to write a novel, the way retired people take up golf. On the first page of a new pad, he had noted down:

Father and Father Away
Keeping Mum
With Dog as my Witness
The Chronicle of Serious Burns

He never got beyond the titles. It had done him good, all the same. The most he had composed over the last two years was a few postcards, and that had been hard enough. He was scared of words. Even in speech, he used them as sparingly as possible. They belonged to another life, that of a small-time journalist reporting what passed for news – stolen ducks, sinks, mopeds – for the local rag. But since he and Odile had been running the perfume shop, he only needed to call upon about forty words of vocabulary: 'Good morning, Madame', 'Goodbye, Madame' and so on.

*

A voice with a distinct garlic whiff of Provençal announced the train's arrival in the capital. One by one the passengers awoke from their trance, lowing like cows at milking time. Those who had been dying of boredom fifteen minutes earlier were now marvelling at the phenomenal speed of the TGV. The woman with the photos shot him a brilliant smile and the thick-set skinhead seemed to thicken further. Everyone was preparing to return to normal life and talking about the extreme temperatures that would greet them on the platform at Gare de Lyon.

'They're saying it's minus fifteen!'

'Minus seventeen, I heard!'

Olivier had always found his mother to be a pain in the neck. But dying a few days before Christmas, in Versailles, at minus seventeen degrees? That was something else.

The view from the window changed from fields to suburban houses, to four-storey buildings, to tower blocks. A few minutes later, Olivier was in Paris.

His hands thrust into the pockets of his parka right up to his elbow, Roland had been pacing up and down the concourse at Gare Saint-Lazare for half an hour. His left ear was still burning from the blow he had received. He was struggling to calm down. He could still see the stunned looks on the faces of the children who had witnessed the bust-up outside Galeries Lafayette: 'The Father Christmases too!' Roland and the other guy had been at one another's throats like two hookers fighting for turf. Their respective photographers had eventually managed to pull them apart. The other guy had blood all over his white beard, which was hanging round his neck like a napkin. Roland's beard was lost entirely. Monsieur Lopez, his photographer, had called him every name under the sun while he got changed in the toilets at Havre–Caumartin. That was where poor sods like him put on the traditional red outfit and cotton-wool beard on top of their own questionable clothing. Despite the torn hood, he managed to squeeze a hundred francs out of Lopez. He had really screwed up losing this job on day one. That hundred francs was all he had to his name.

He had instinctively fled to Gare Saint-Lazare because he had nowhere to go, and people with nowhere to go always end up at stations. If there was one thing he knew about, it was stations. He had spent three months playing deaf and dumb on commuter trains. One day he had come across a bag filled with a hundred or so Mickey Mouse key rings and the same number of pin badges, along with a card certifying that the bearer was deaf and dumb and authorised to sell on the SNCF rail network. He had kept his mouth shut for three months, until he had a run-in with a sour-tempered ticket inspector.

A succession of other roles followed, with Roland always playing against type . . . It was almost ten past midnight. It was so cold that the air seemed to have solidified. The travellers had doubled in volume, bundled up in layers of jumpers, scarves and coats. Puffs of steam emerged from their mouths, making them look like little factories. Roland had only been on earth for twenty-two years but it already felt too long. He would have liked to be adopted, if only for Christmas, by any one of those standing on the platform, stamping their feet to keep warm while checking the time on their watches.

Roland exchanged a few words and a cigarette with another homeless man as mangy as the dog by his side. The station was almost empty. Roland was as lonely as the ball inside a jingle bell. He jumped on the last train. It was going to Versailles.

Of all the foreign languages whirling in the air beneath the pyramid at the Louvre, Italian predominated. It was as if the Medicis had come back to house-sit for the holidays. Shivering, bundled up in scarves, they were talking even more loudly than usual to keep warm, and their sunny accents were a strange contrast to the arctic conditions prevailing in Paris.

Rodolphe had been forced to queue among them for a good half-hour before entering the museum. He felt like a lettuce heart left to wilt in the drawer at the bottom of the fridge. He resembled one of those blocks of lard sculpted into the shape of an animal and placed in the windows of the best charcuteries. A pig, for example, a lovely little pink pig with black glasses and a funny face as if squinting at the sun.

In Rodolphe's case, it was not the sun but an eternal eclipse that clamped that strained smile on his fat face. In common with all blind people, he seemed to face the sky expectantly, chin raised as if preparing for take-off, tethered to the ground only by the tip of his telescopic stick.

Every time he entered the room where *The Raft of the Medusa* hung, he felt as if he was arriving at a ball, with footsteps on the wooden floor and whispers swirling around him, the only music the rustling of fabric and bodies brushing past one another. With a flick of the wrist he folded up his white stick and strode confidently to the bench in the middle of the room. There was no need to invoke his disability to get a seat since no one was sitting there. Rodolphe plonked down his one hundred and twenty kilos of weight, peeled off his overcoat, jacket and cardigan like a giant onion, then laid his chubby little hands flat against his enormous thighs and waited, giving a grunt of pleasure.

As his body slowly warmed and loosened up, he clung to life like a ball of soft dough. One by one he felt his pores opening, millions of little hungry mouths greedily sucking up every little sound, smell and vibration around him. The crowds were his plankton and he wallowed among them as a basking seal.

A very small woman of a certain age perched on the bench alongside him. She smelt of biscuits and eau de Cologne.

'Excuse me, Madame. Do you speak French?'

'Yes.'

'Oh, good. Would you mind telling me about the painting there, in front of us?'

'*The Raft of the Medusa*?'

'That's the one!'

'But . . . What do you want me to tell you?'

'I'm visually impaired and . . .'

'Oh! I'm sorry, I hadn't noticed. You don't often come across bli—, visually impaired people in galleries.'

'I appreciate why you might be surprised, Madame, but I'm waiting for my sister to come and pick me up. I can still enjoy something of the art through other people's eyes. As long as I'm not bothering you?'

'No, not at all! So . . . it's a picture of a raft . . . with people on it, far out at sea.'

'Ah.'

'Just a minute, I've got a guide . . . Géricault, Géricault . . . Ah, here we are. *The Raft of the Medusa*, 1819, acquired in 1824—'

'No, I'm not interested in that. I want to know what *you* can see.'

'What I can see?'

'Yes. How many people are on this raft? Is it day or night? Colours, everything!'

'Right, right. Hang on, I'm counting them . . . The thing is, some of them are dead and some alive.'

'Count the bodies, just the bodies!'

'I'd say about fifteen but I can't be sure, they're all piled up . . .'

'Is it disgusting?'

'No! Well, actually yes, a bit. It's tragic, isn't it?'

'It's tragic . . . and is it day or night?'

'Neither. It could be dawn or dusk . . .'

'Which do you think?'

'Dusk.'

'Ah, the gloaming! It's a terrible time of day, isn't it? You know it's nearly over but you don't know when it's going to end, only that it will. It's terrible not knowing, isn't it? Excuse me.'

Rodolphe took from his pocket a huge handkerchief almost the size of a sail and blew his nose loudly. The little old lady shrank slightly further away.

'I beg your pardon. So what are they doing, these people on the raft?'

'Well, er . . . some of them are dead and half covered in water, and others are waving their shirts in the air for help.'

'Who from?'

'That, I don't know. They're doing it to keep their hopes up.'

'To keep their hopes up? What are you talking about? You told me they were stranded way out at sea . . . You shouldn't take advantage of my disability to lead me up the garden path!'

'I'm not, I swear!'

'OK, if they're calling for help, it means there's a boat somewhere. Use your eyes, damn it!'

'Ah, yes, yes! I can see a boat actually, but it's very small, just a dot on the horizon.'

'So they're going to be saved?'

'Yes, they'll be saved.'

'No.'

'Why not?'

'Because that's the boat that abandoned them. There were two ships in this story. One of them – the *Medusa* – sank. The survivors were piled onto a raft attached to the other ship, but during the night the rope holding them together snapped or – more likely – was cut. No one ever knew for certain. So it's not dusk, it's dawn. These poor sods have just realised they've been cut adrift. Oh no! They're going to start eating each other, and some of them will get a taste for it. They'll drink their own piss.

13

Some is better than others, apparently. Did you know that?'

'No.'

'Oh yes, there's good piss and bad piss. Hope has the flavour of piss and rotting flesh. Had you never noticed?'

'No, I . . . I should be going . . .'

'Wait. You mustn't give up hope, even if it reeks of urine and decaying corpses. The proof is that there were three survivors.'

'Oh really?'

'Yes, three, including the shipwright Corréard. He's the one you can see to the right of the sail, pointing to the horizon.'

'How do you know that?'

'I met his great-grandson. And do you know how this brave shipwright died?'

'No.'

'Drowned in a puddle a few years later, bladdered after a barn dance in Normandy.'

'Why are you telling me this?'

'To remind you there's always someone looking out for you up there.'

He listened gleefully to the old lady's footsteps hurrying towards the exit. As often as he could, Rodolphe arranged to be dropped at the Louvre where he would make a beeline for Géricault's painting and tell his anecdote to the first French-speaking person to sit next to him. His story made the greatest impression on the elderly, like the woman who had just scurried off. By the time they reached old age, people always had a few regrets, and had seen others carried off for the most minor of sins; they felt preyed upon, and they were.

'Survivors, ha! Silly bitch. Life leaves no survivors.'

People tended to forget this and act as if they were immortal, and Rodolphe took it upon himself to remind them. He did this not only for the pleasure of spoiling their day – though the sour smell of fear did bring him some satisfaction – but because he felt himself invested with a public service mission: 'No use playing tough: you're being watched and we'll all pay our debts in the end.'

He really had met the descendant of the *Medusa*'s shipwright in a bar five years earlier. He was one of those drunks who over the course of an evening give away a family secret, or rather spill it into their glass. To Rodolphe, the story was a revelation. It was his duty to pass it on. Was destiny not as blind as him, after all?

Though he did not speak Italian, he gathered people were talking about food, and a gong sounded from his stomach. He had arranged to meet Jeanne at one o'clock and it was now quarter to. Jeanne was always on time but since he was always early, it was as if she was always late. He was already feeling annoyed with her.

Since that morning, Jeanne had seen three dwarves: the first on her way out of Versailles, on Avenue de Paris, the second while dropping her brother off outside the Louvre and the third, a woman, shopping at La Samaritaine. Some days are like that. Other days, you keep seeing film actors or bumping into people you haven't seen for a long time, or take the same taxi twice, or nothing happens at all.

She was looking for a gift for Rodolphe but had no idea what to get. She would rather not give him anything, if she was honest. He had been even more odious than normal recently. But it was Christmas, and even naughty children were entitled to a present. She eventually opted for a set of bathroom scales, an unequivocally tasteless object covered in brown velour with a brass rim, Jules Verne style. It was a completely useless gift since Rodolphe didn't care two hoots about his obesity and would not be able to see the reading anyway. But it was heavy and came in a big box, so it would make a nice present.

Having made her selection, she could not resist a look at

the toy section, in spite of the swarms of harassed parents and overexcited children. All the dolls looked as if they had walked out of horror films, they were so alarmingly lifelike. Some had teeth and spoke inane words with metallic voices. It was terrifying. The dolls of her childhood did not speak, eat, wee or poo. They were either stiff or floppy. The first black doll went on sale when she was twelve. She was sorry not to have had one, but it was too late by then. That was the age she became old overnight. One morning she got up and her toys no longer spoke to her. They had become objects, things. She touched them, turned them over in her hands as though seeing them for the first time, and began to cry. Her childhood had run away during the night.

The pistols, rifles and submachine guns for boys looked more authentic than the real things. The kids were trying them out for size, making them rattle into action with expert ease. A mini Sarajevo. Had a terrorist slipped a real weapon among them, there would have been utter carnage. This was a truly false world. Anything could be forged, everything could be questioned; calves were being cloned and one could not even be sure of remaining the same person from one day to the next. Plagiarism had become the ultimate, fatal art form and illusion the universal religion.

Jeanne couldn't care less. What was wrong with sending a cloned Jeanne to work and to pick up Rodolphe from the Louvre? What would she do with herself in the meantime? Nothing. She would be dead and thanks to her double, everyone would think she was still alive.

A child came along and threw himself at her legs. He already had the face of an old codger. With twenty years of teaching behind her, nothing surprised Jeanne any more. She had loved kids and then hated them, and now she was as indifferent to them as she was to adults. It was just a case of putting up with them and waving them away like flies from time to time.

As Jeanne left the department store carrying the scales under her arm, the cold air struck her full in the face, in stark contrast to the stifling heat inside La Samaritaine. For a few seconds it took her breath away. She didn't actually mind this weather – the coldest since the winter of 1917 – any more than she had the heat wave the previous summer. She liked extremes. It was the same with dwarves: they were out of the ordinary.

She arrived in the room containing *The Raft of the Medusa* at exactly one o'clock. Rodolphe looked peeved.

'It's me.'

'Yes, I know it's you. You should change your perfume, then I could imagine I was meeting someone else.'

'What difference would it make? You don't like anybody.'

'That's not true. It's them that don't like me.'

'Well, I like you. How about a nice *choucroute*?'

It was all yellow, the yellow of old teeth which would soon turn brown. But it was clean, perfectly maintained by Madeleine, his mother's cleaning lady. She was the one who had found her a few days earlier, lying in bed with her hands clutching the edge of the sheets and her eyes eternally trained on a crack in the ceiling in the shape of Corsica.

Dead people don't decorate the way we do. They put crocheted doilies with pineapple or spiral patterns all over the place – on top of the TV, underneath the phone, draped over cushions like spiders' webs. Olivier was unsure where to put himself in the cramped, overheated flat he was setting foot in for the first time. Certain items of furniture and ornaments were familiar from his childhood, like the little writing desk he used to like to hide under. On its right foot, you could still see the mark where a pedal car had crashed into it. Or the brass lamp shade his father had proudly brought home one night, a gift from a client. These recollections aside, everything was foreign to him.

On her husband's death, Olivier's mother had sold the house in Le Chesnay and moved into this small one bedroom flat. 'Now that I'm *all on my own*' (and she had really emphasised the 'all on my own') 'it's plenty big enough for me.'

She would no doubt have liked Olivier to be up in arms at the idea of selling the family home, but in fact he couldn't care less. He had completely wiped Versailles from the map.

Getting off the train two hours earlier at the gloomy, silent, freezing Gare Rive Droite, he had been surprised to feel nothing at all. It could have been any other provincial town, curled up in its shell, hiding from the cold and dark. He was relieved, because he had been approaching his reunion with the place with a degree of apprehension. It was silly to have worried; after all, it was only stone, cobbles and bricks. And yet nothing had changed. Looking out of the window of the taxi taking him to his mother's home, he recognised everything, even if a few shops had changed hands. The lead-coloured avenues and boulevards fanning out from Place d'Armes in front of the chateau were still the same. A quilt of snow softened the street corners and padded the pavements. Versailles was wearing a wig. He had been to pick up the keys from Madeleine, whom his mother had often talked about, but whom he had never met.

From the moment they laid eyes on one another, he could see she had hated him for a long time.

'Oh, Monsieur Olivier, you look so much like her! My sincere condolences, Monsieur Olivier. It's so sad! Excuse me.'

She plunged her nose (which looked like a rancid hunk of Gruyère) into a handful of tissues, while continuing to give him the evil eye. She was much as he had pictured her, voluntarily enslaved, even more of a Versaillaise than her mistress. A by-product. She had insisted on coming with him to the home of his 'poor maman', whom he sadly could not see until the next day because the undertakers had transferred the body to the morgue.

The trouble was, with the weather like this and the Christmas holidays approaching, people were dying in large numbers. The funeral might not be held until the 26th or even 27th.

'The 27th?'

'That's what they told me!'

For a good half-hour she carried on about his poor mother's poor armchair, his poor mother's poor mirror, his poor mother's poor life. All the above swam in a poor whiff of poor leeks.

'Thanks for everything, Madeleine. If you'll excuse me, I'm rather tired ...'

'Of course, you poor thing, I understand. I'll leave you to your memories. If you need anything at all ...'

'That's very kind of you, Madeleine. Thanks again.'

Everything he touched had been touched by the hand of a dead person and he found the idea vaguely disgusting, even if that person was his mother. He wondered where he was going to sleep. Not in the bed, that was for sure. Tomorrow he would look for a hotel, but he didn't have the strength to go out again in the bitter cold tonight, roaming this ghost town in search of a place to stay. The sofa, maybe? Curling up like a winkle, he should fit. He plumped up the cushions and removed the ubiquitous lace doilies from the arms. Before anything else, he must call Odile to let her know he had arrived safely and that proceedings might be delayed.

What had the old bat been talking about, having the funeral on the 26th or 27th? It was the 21st today. A whole week to kill here! She must have got her wires crossed. Either she was losing the plot or was saying it to wind him up because she couldn't bear him. He could just picture his mother leaning on Madeleine's bony shoulder and pouring her heart out. 'Ungrateful child ... cast me aside like an old apple ...' That was exactly what he should have done instead of having her down on the coast with them for a fortnight every August. She was never satisfied, always putting Odile down, constantly criticising and complaining – her legs, her shoulders, her head, off with her head … No doubt the two old biddies exchanged notes on everything. He would find out for himself tomorrow.

It was an old telephone with finger-holes, covered in garnet-red velour with an elegant trim of gold braid. The receiver smelt of dried spit.

'Odile? It's me.'

'How are you? Did you get there OK?'

'Yes, I'm here now. How are you?'

'I'm OK, but it's getting a bit much. Have you seen how busy it is everywhere? Mireille came to give me a hand. She said she'd help out until you get back.'

'About that … the funeral might not happen until the 26th or 27th.'

'What? What do you mean?'

'Calm down. It was Madeleine who said it but she's completely insane; I'm sure she's got the wrong end of the stick.'

'I certainly hope so! What am I going to do with the shop? And we said we were going to spend Christmas—'

'Do you think I want to be stuck here? Listen, don't worry. Tomorrow I'm going to the undertaker's, I'll ring Emmaus to get the flat cleared, I'll swing by the lawyer and then I'll be on the first train or plane out of here. I just want to get back. Believe me, this whole thing's a total pain.'

'I know, darling. I love you.'

'I love you too. Right, I'd better see if I can find something to eat.'

'Will you call me tomorrow?'

'Of course. Speak then, darling. Love you lots.'

'You too, speak tomorrow.'

People who love each other always say, 'You too, speak tomorrow.'

After putting the phone down, he felt terribly lonely. The sound of Odile's voice floating in his ears underlined the oddness of the situation. It was the first time they had been apart for more than twenty-four hours since they got married. There was something bizarre about parachuting into another life – if you could call this empty flat a life. He had long since scrumpled all family ties into a ball and chucked it over his shoulder. His mother must have made doilies out of hers. He had no memory of them ever having loved one another. It was Odile who had insisted, 'Olivier, she was still your mother!' What did 'still-a-mother' mean? It was like 'a-father-after-all', 'parents-can't-live-without-'em', or 'a-baby-yes-why-not?' He had not come up when his father died. A family for a fortnight a year ... The hand that feeds you. Hunger forced him to pull himself together.

More than anywhere else in the flat, the kitchen glowed yellowish like the colour of nicotine-stained teeth; even the sink enamel looked like old ivory. The fridge was empty and had been unplugged. All he could find to eat was a bottle of Viandox sauce at the back of a cupboard and half a packet of alphabet pasta for soups. Before he closed the cupboard door, the alluring label of an almost full bottle of Negrita caught his eye. He shrugged and put a saucepan of water on to boil.

'Rodolphe, will you stop that?'

'What's the matter, don't want anyone to see you sulking?'

'I'm not sulking. You're annoying me with the camcorder. Stop it, please.'

Rodolphe put the camera down beside a plate on which a piece of cheese rind and an end crust of bread were languishing. The low-hanging ceiling lamp held the table in a cone of orange light. Jeanne was sitting in one of the two identical armchairs facing the TV. With her back turned to her brother, she was haloed by the bluish rays of the screen. The rest of the room was plunged in darkness.

'You've started getting so high and mighty, making a fuss whenever I try to film you.'

'Don't be silly. It's just irritating to feel someone's eye on you all the time.'

'A blind man's eye!'

'An eye all the same. It produces images.'

'But you said you liked my films.'

'I do, but I'm fed up with being your only star and having to look at myself from every angle.'

'You're missing the point. I'm filming the sounds, not you.'

'I must be making too much noise then. I'm in every shot.'

'It's you who puts yourself in every frame. You've always been full of yourself.'

'Will you let me watch the TV?'

'You see! Self-obsessed, stuck up and snooty.'

'I'm getting tired of this, Rodolphe.'

'You're tireless.'

'Don't believe that for a second.'

For a moment the only sound was the humming of the television, a programme presented by media whores who did nothing but talk about themselves with no regard for the people watching. That was fine because neither Jeanne nor Rodolphe nor anyone else in the world was interested in them either. Even though brother and sister had their backs to one another, a sense of an impending face-off filled the room. Rodolphe stretched his hand out above the table, found the bottle of wine and poured himself a glass, stopping as if by miracle just before it overflowed.

'What does that mean: "Don't believe that for a second"?'

'You've had enough to drink this evening.'

Rodolphe downed the glass in one. A drip ran down his chin. He wiped it away with his finger.

'What does that mean: "Don't believe that for a second"?'

'It means you're getting more and more temperamental and demanding, and if you carry on like this, I'm going to leave.'

'Leave? ... Where?'

'Anywhere, somewhere quiet.'

'There's no such place. You'd really drop me, just like that?'

'Of course. I'd come and see you on Sundays.'

'Sundays ... My whole childhood, I only ever saw you on Sundays.'

'Well, I was at boarding school, wasn't I?'

'You still are. You live in your own little world, filing your little things neatly away. You live life to the minimum, like a prisoner. Maybe I've become more of a pain in the arse, but you've put up thicker defences. Sometimes I wonder if you're not ... it shocks me to say it ... happy!'

'I'm not unhappy.'

They said nothing more. Rodolphe sat down beside her and immediately dozed off. He slept like a log. The baddie in the TV series that had come on after the talk show looked a bit like him: a smooth, pink-faced doll at a jumble sale. Rodolphe had become what he had always been, a big whingeing nuisance of a baby. Jeanne was the only one who could put up with him. She put up with everything, a caryatid holding up a sky that constantly threatened to cave in. It was a job like any other; there was no virtue in it, she just got on with it. Rodolphe was right, she was tireless, because she put no value on what she did. She lit a cigarette. She smoked too much, was smoking more and more, a little smoke machine. She looked at her hands in the glow of the Bic lighter and did not recognise them. They picked up the cigarette, brought it to her mouth, rested on her knees, drummed their fingertips. Her hands had a life of their own; they had no need of her. Only Rodolphe needed her, but she needed no one, not Rodolphe, not her hands. Just cigarettes, that was all. She wasn't unhappy exactly, but she wasn't happy either.

She was Jeanne, an indestructible block of Jeanne apparently able to last for ever, standing flawlessly alone, her military demeanour no doubt inherited from her father, Colonel Mangin, who had fallen in battle somewhere on the other side of the world. She was twelve when he was killed, and his death made no impact on her. All through her childhood, the man with a constant tan and a crew cut had only hung around long enough to bark a few brief orders before disappearing again once he was satisfied they had been obeyed. One morning, two gendarmes came to the door. Her mother went pale reading the letter. The twins, Xavier and Denis, her eighteen-year-old big brothers, held their mother up and told Jeanne to go and look after Rodolphe. The only thing left of all this was a yellowed photo showing the hard-edged soldier smiling in front of a tank with sand dunes in the distance, in a fake lizard-skin frame in Rodolphe's bedroom.

'Look after your brother!'

She had heard the same thing again and again throughout her

childhood, a kind of refrain which was put on pause when the fuss happened and resumed fifteen years later, after boarding school, after the École normale, when her mother and the twins perished in a car accident on the way to Saint-Cyr military academy. She felt nothing then either. Neither the wizened vine stock of a mother nor her two idiot sons with skulls moulded by their army-issue kepis had left any kind of hole in her life.

Propelled by some instinct, she left her job as an English teacher in Melun and came back to Versailles to look after Rodolphe, who was stubbornly refusing to take responsibility for himself. They sold the flat in Le Chesnay and moved close to Gare Rive Gauche, more convenient for getting to Viroflay where she had found work at a private school. She was thirty at the time; she would be forty at the beginning of February, an age when one might wish at last to stand alone in the world. Now there was only emptiness to fill her up.

Everything had begun to go tits up the day he was born, much as it had for the scrawny Christ dying of boredom in the empty church of Notre-Dame de Versailles. Waking him around seven o'clock that morning, the priest had given Roland a bowl of coffee and a limp *tartine*, which he wolfed down, and then asked him to stay put and pray. He would be back with warm clothes, perhaps even a bit of money, but after that Roland really would have to leave. He was still young, he had so much to look forward to, he could build himself a proper life like other people, but he must do it somewhere else. He just had to roll up his sleeves and ... Roland did not listen to the rest of this off-the-cuff sermon. The words tinkled under the rib vaults like ice cubes in the bottom of a glass. The priest just wanted to get rid of him. Preparations were afoot for midnight mass and there was no role for him in the Nativity. The scene was coloured khaki, grey, black and brown, with a few hopeful glimmers of gold here and there.

Roland thought the frescos and sculptures representing hell were a hundred times more appealing than the pale, cold depictions of heaven. He had no time for either of them anyway. The only thing he was interested in was how much cash the priest was going to give him. A hundred? He was also wondering what the podgy cherubs flitting above his head would taste like, spit-roasted like suckling pigs. The morning's lukewarm coffee and soggy bread had filled a hole but left him unsatisfied. Did people imagine the poor could not tell the difference between a shitty *tartine* and a *choucroute garnie*, between a tatty old jumper and a cashmere sweater?

After leaving the station the previous night, he had headed to the church of Notre-Dame on Rue de la Paroisse, which was of course shut. God keeps set hours, after all. He skirted the building before hunkering down outside the presbytery door. It was a good place to die. The road was as empty as a dieting secretary's fridge. He scrunched himself up like a letter destined for the bin – 'Dear God, it has come to my attention …' – and waited for the cold to set in. His brain shrank to a compact block with a vague image of his eight-year-old self suspended in the middle, like those lumps of resin with insects trapped inside that people use as paperweights. Then the priest arrived, red-faced, wrapped up in a bulky sheepskin coat and a woolly hat, his arms laden with packages.

'What are you doing here, my child?'

Through frozen lips, Roland stuttered something like, 'I'm dying, Monsieur, I'm dying …'

The priest looked around, as if caught doing something he shouldn't.

'This isn't really the place for it … I mean …'

What he meant was that it wasn't proper, that it would attract vermin, that sort of thing. He was clearly uncomfortable with the situation, but what else could he do?

'Help me carry all this into the sacristy.'

'Can't, M'sieur, can't move.'

The priest muttered something that sounded awfully like a profanity, put down his packages and opened the door.

'Come, my child. Come in.'

Roland slowly followed him inside. The warmth melted him. It was green and smelt of incense and old cardboard, like Aunt Margot's house in Rouen.

'Sit yourself down. I'll make you a coffee.'

Why the obsession with giving coffee to the poor, the drowned, the suicides …

The priest asked him if he was Christian, if he had read the Bible, in short, if his papers were in order. Roland said yes to everything, nodding his head like an ass for convenience. All he wanted was to lie down and go to sleep – for ever, if possible.

'Right, OK, well, you can stay the night, but that's all. Theoretically …'

'Yes.'

'Tomorrow I'll give you some addresses, some names of people who can help you.'

'Yes.'

'You're lucky I came by with my … Can I trust you?'

'Yes.'

'Good. Well, good night then.'

'Yes.'

There is such a thing as a full 'yes', like full nudity. The night was full too, dreamless, heavy, leaden, like nights of old.

Someone entered the church. The sound of footsteps preceded by a tap-tap. Someone with a stick.

That old fossil Madeleine was right. The burial could not take place before the 27th; the undertaker had just told him so. The dead just kept coming and the ground was rock-hard.

'What if we had her cremated?'

'Monsieur! We must respect the deceased's last wishes. Your mother had planned for everything.'

'Except dying at Christmas. So there's nothing we can do?'

'I'm afraid not.'

However careful the undertaker was to disguise his true feelings, Olivier was sure that he too took him for an ungrateful child. He followed the man to the coffin in which his mother lay, as woefully small and insignificant in death as she had been in life, clothed in a violet dress and plastered in ridiculous make-up with a fixed smile, a fungal tangle of white hair on her scalp and bony hands crossed over her belly as though trying to abort herself.

He went straight from the undertaker's to the train station to check the timetable. He was prepared to leave and come back again two days later, anything to avoid hanging around in this shithole. There was an unusual amount of kerfuffle, people gesticulating at ticket counters or spinning disoriented on the spot like mechanical toys. He was told there were no trains running on any of the main lines because of the icy conditions, and he had no chance of catching a plane either.

'So I have to wait until it thaws?'

'That's right.'

For a brief moment he felt like hanging himself. The whole

thing was so absurd, trapped in the ice fields of Versailles! He didn't know where to start: phone Odile to pass on all this good news? Make an appointment with the lawyer? With Emmaus?

What was the point? He was sure whatever he did would end in disaster.

On Rue Carnot a bulb had blown on one of the stars in the Christmas lights, making it appear to be squinting. People emerged from shops transformed into porters carrying trees, bags, enormous boxes tied with string, gift-wrapped parcels with ribbon around them which would be clogging up dustbins within days, the contents tumbling noisily down the rubbish chute. Freshly trussed turkeys, bloodstained boar's legs, fat geese, pyramids of snails and monstrous turds of white pudding came spewing out of butchers and charcuteries – the sight of it was enough to give you indigestion. People bought any old rubbish at any old price, committing a kind of budgetary suicide with the most tenuous of links to the birth of the baby Jesus. There was a general desire to end it all, drowning in bad champagne and foie gras from Monoprix.

Olivier let himself be jostled this way and that, feeling dazed and detached from his body. During the festive season, Versailles sparkled with inevitability. On Avenue de Saint-Cloud the crowd began to thin out. Unconsciously, his feet were leading him towards Lycée Hoche where he had gone to school between the ages of eleven and fourteen. As he got closer, he tried to recall the names of his teachers and classmates. Some of them came back to him: Monsieur Mauduit, Madame Le Breton, Vidal, Joly, Langlois ... He saw himself too, satchel bulging with heavy textbooks, exercise books and gym kit, waiting for bus B ... His mind was warming up but he felt as if he was delving into someone else's memories.

His first death had come the year he turned fourteen and he had not stopped dying and being reborn ever since. Amazing –

only in Versailles could you see the words 'Long Live the King!' graffitied on the school walls. The front gates were locked but he could see through them to the dome of the chapel across the main courtyard, where pupils and teachers gathered to lift the flag every 11 November. The cassowary feathers of the Saint-Cyrien cadets hung limply in the inevitable rain. He was sorry not to feel anything at all. Funny the lengths the brain goes to in order to protect the body.

He began walking back into town by way of Rue de la Paroisse and stopped to warm up in a café on Place du Marché. Since giving up drink, he never knew what to order. He didn't feel like a coffee, and couldn't make up his mind between a Viandox and a tomato juice. With a dash of Tabasco, tomato juice was the beverage that most resembled alcohol. For the first time in ages, he really fancied a drink. He put too much Tabasco in and made himself choke. All around him, people were talking too loudly, laughing annoyingly. Since his teens, he had never loved anyone. Since then, he had never been anything but a pleasant yet indifferent passenger through life. Odile didn't ask for more, which explained why they got on so well. In conversation, he played his cards close to his chest. People either took him for a snob or a harmless idiot, or both. It was all the same to him.

Was it the incongruity of the situation, or had he spent too long outside Lycée Hoche? He felt ill at ease, on edge, as if haunted by something he could not control. He struggled to get a grip on himself. The transition from the arctic conditions outside to the warmth of the café had been abrupt … Was he coming down with a fever? That was all he needed. He gritted his teeth, mentally shook himself and left the café.

Jeanne had spent all day lying around in her dressing gown and slippers with a cigarette hanging from her mouth, grazing on fruit, keeping one eye on the TV and the other on a trashy detective novel. She loved duvet days. Rodolphe had left early that morning and not been back since. Around four o'clock, she finally decided it was time for a bath. Standing in front of the mirror with wet hair slicked either side of her sharp-featured face, she thought she bore a resemblance to Cruella De Vil, who would soon be making her annual onscreen appearance as the Christmas holidays loomed. She was not troubled by the likeness to a baddie. In fact she felt a certain degree of pride in belonging to the family of reprobates denounced in films and novels. They alone carried the misery of the world on their shoulders, and in her eyes they were a hundred times more worthy of respect than the fresh-faced heroes who moulded God in their own image. She, however, was not cruel. Her pupils judged her strict but fair, and her colleagues courteous but cold.

She had gone from being slim to skinny, as others went from chubby to fat. And yet she denied herself nothing, had a healthy appetite and was rarely ill – the odd cold, nothing serious. Food just went straight through her. She asked herself how long it had been since she last had sex, but could not answer. Years … Sometimes in dreams. Her belly had always been flat and would remain so, her bony hips sticking out either side. People said men preferred women with a bit of meat on them. That was rubbish; they liked whatever they could get. She didn't hold it against them, not that she had been with many: three, including a teenager and a woman she spent almost a year with. Fanchon was headmistress of the secondary school in Melun, the man a BNP bank clerk in the same town, and the teenager, the first …

The hairbrush fell out of her hands. The stale whiff of the past wafted back to her only very rarely. She made do with living in an eternal present, odourless, colourless and tasteless. The hairdryer put her thoughts back in order, a great gust of wind blasting through her head.

'A drowned rat', that was how the twins used to describe her.

They had no more weight on them than she did; lean and tough, like their father – and their mother. Rodolphe was the odd one out. He had gone from being a fat baby to a fat little boy and grew up to become obese. Was it linked to his blindness? That was a mystery to chew over. Like all children, he first started exploring the world with his mouth, and had never stopped. As soon as he was introduced to someone, he would smack his flabby, sugar-coated lips against their cheek like a suction cup, hoovering them into his wide-open mouth. Children were afraid of him. But Rodolphe was not an intrinsically bad person. It was only repeated rejection that had made him that way. Sometimes she wished he would die, for his own good. Unlike her, he could not bear the solitude nature had inflicted on him. But despite the layer of fat strangling it, his heart carried on mercilessly beating.

Jeanne had just put on a jumper and a pair of black trousers when the doorbell rang.

'Hi, I'm your neighbour, or rather, your neighbour's son, and I …'

Olivier shrank back. The black pupils in the eyes of the woman who had just opened the door to him looked like two great lead wrecking balls. An entire wall of his past went crashing to the ground, leaving nothing behind it.

'Have we met?'

No matter how prepared you are, there are some things you cannot see coming. Jeanne was face to face with Olivier. An Olivier disguised as a respectable gentleman with salt and pepper hair, dressed in a suit and tie, but Olivier all the same. She could not speak or make a sound, but two beads of salt water began welling beneath her eyelids. The man standing before her wobbled as if gripped with vertigo.

'I don't believe it … Jeanne?'

'Come in.'

This was not real life in the everyday world where you could come and go as you pleased; Olivier knew what a massive step he was taking. This was not a matter of chance. What it was a matter of, he did not know. He had set foot on a slippery slope and he was sliding, yes, sliding. He had come round to ask his neighbour for the phone book and found himself face to face with his past, with Jeanne, his Jeanne, the Jeanne of his youth, with whom his life had turned upside down, and again he felt knocked off balance. It was scary and wonderful all at once.

'Sit down.'

Olivier fell back onto a sofa. He couldn't take anything in. The smell of soap and shampoo wafted from Jeanne, who had hardly changed after all these years. He felt the urge to laugh; the whole thing was so unlikely, it was as if he had dreamed it.

'I ... I don't know what to say.'

'Don't say anything.'

There he was, in front of her. He was there. He wasn't dead. He was crossing and uncrossing his legs. He had wrinkles, white hair, a tic that made the corner of his mouth twitch, but he was there. The past lay ahead of her, opening its closets to reveal the resident skeletons ...

'Do you want something to drink?'

'No, thank you. It's so ... What are you doing here?'

'What are *you* doing here?'

He could have told her his mother had died and he had come up for the funeral, but he settled for raising his eyebrows as if to say, 'Beats me.' There clearly was a reason for his being here, but putting it into words was beyond him. It was the same for Jeanne: the whys and wherefores seemed superfluous, they were there, after ...

'How long has it been?'

'A long time.'

Jeanne had settled into an armchair opposite Olivier and

sat facing him, hugging her knees. They stayed looking at one another like two mirrors eternally returning the other's reflection.

They had overcome their initial shock. Now they were facing reality. The child was still intact in both of them, dazzling like a pure diamond. Time had stood still and they were holding their breath as if underwater. Olivier felt his heart implode. He closed his eyes and threw his head back, clutching his brow.

'Fuck! … Fuck me!'

They were not so much words as a sort of rattle.

'I'll make some coffee.'

Jeanne was no longer sitting in the armchair but he could hear her moving utensils about in the kitchen. She would soon return to sit in front of him. What would he say to her? 'So, what do you do these days? … You haven't changed a bit … Can you believe this cold? … What's for dinner? … Did you see whatsit's last film? … Oh yes please, I will have a bit more mash …' Maybe not, but he was going to have to say something. The room looked like any other lounge: sofa, armchair, table, chairs, rug and lamp. No mirror. It was all a bit dull and unimaginative, clean and functional, just what was needed and no more. Only a print of *The Raft of the Medusa* on one wall. The curtains were drawn. The room probably didn't see daylight very often. Jeanne must have inherited the furniture; it wasn't what you would choose. She returned carrying a tray.

'You live on your own?'

'No.'

'Ah …'

'I live with Rodolphe.'

'Your brother?'

'Yes. My mother and the twins died in a car accident. Rodolphe can't manage on his own. Do you take sugar?'

'No, thanks. My mother has just died, that's why I'm here.'

'The old lady across the hall?'

'Yes.'

'That's funny, I'd noticed her surname on the letter box but I thought it must be a coincidence. I didn't recognise her. To tell the truth, I only bumped into her once or twice. She hardly ever went out.'

'So you left Le Chesnay?'

'Yes. It suits us better here. We've got two of everything – two toilets, two bathrooms – it's a bit like two separate flats. Having said that, Rodolphe spends most of his time in my half. What about you, where do you live?'

'On the coast, in Nice.'

'Are you married?'

'Yes, I got married two years ago.'

He blushed, as if caught doing something wrong, as if he were cheating.

'So you've come back for the funeral.'

'That's right. But it's been put back because of the holidays … because of the weather … Long and short of it, I'm stuck here until the 27th. The reason I came round was to borrow a phone book. I need to call Emmaus to clear the flat.'

'I'll dig one out.'

There, everything was back to normal, life had resumed its ordinary course. They drank coffee and chatted, sharing minor gripes and moans. The marionettes were once again jiggling on their strings. Olivier put his cup down on the tray a little too hard and clasped his face in his hands.

'Jeanne! Jeanne, do you know what this means?'

He had said the same thing twenty-five years earlier and, just like then, she could only reply, 'That's the way it is. There's nothing we can do.'

'What have you been doing all these years?'

'The same as always, I think. The days, months and years

35

followed on smoothly from one another. After you left, I was sent to boarding school and then I took an English degree. I'm a teacher. That's all there is to say.'

'Did you never try to trace me?'

'No. You neither?'

'No. I wanted to wipe it all out, forget, pretend nothing ever ... but I never really managed it. After I came back from Réunion, I went to live in the south. I did some journalism, then some drinking ... I gave up two years ago. I just can't believe this. It's been twenty years, but it feels like yesterday.'

'In that case it must have been a bad night's sleep. You look so tired.'

'I guess so. As for you ... How have you stayed so ... smooth? It's crazy, I recognised you straight away.'

'I don't know, I must have refused to get old.'

'Have you ... have you never thought about it since?'

'About what?'

'You know.'

'Sometimes, at the beginning.'

'And when the guy died. You know he died in prison, five years later?'

'Yes, I saw it in the paper.'

'And you thought nothing of it?'

'Is that all you remember?'

'No, of course not, but ...'

It really was as if they had only spent a day apart. She nearly started doing the goat and sheep impressions she was so good at, or pulling faces to make him laugh. Laughing. When they were alone together, it was all they did. Never in front of other people. Everyone thought they were terribly serious for their age; they all remarked on it. It was how they protected themselves. There were other people, and there was them: two worlds which never converged. 'Aren't they good! ... A real little couple!

... They're like two peas in a pod!' And here they were again twenty-five years later, unscathed, with the death of a child and an unfortunate tramp behind them.

With her legs tucked underneath her and her cheek resting on her palm, Jeanne sat smiling at him.

'It's good to see you.'

That was exactly the right thing to say, and Olivier kicked himself for not getting in there first.

'I could murder a drink.'

The man was a total nutter but he had paid for everything since that morning. The role of guide dog was just another job. 'Mind the step, go left, right ...' Some kind of miracle had brought them together. Of course, churches were designed for that sort of thing.

The blind man had come and sat next to Roland. Like all fat people, he was breathing heavily and sweating in spite of the cold. Mid-puff he whispered, 'Do you believe in this stuff?'

'What stuff?'

'Oh, you know, the good Lord, the baby Jesus, the whole lot of them!'

'I don't know. I'm just waiting for the priest.'

The blind man let out a burst of laughter which ended in a coughing fit. He was clearly not in the habit of laughing; the mechanism sounded rusty and false.

'And what do you think the priest's going to do for you?'

'Give me some clothes, maybe a bit of money.'

'Clothes? No problem, they've got bins overflowing with them, but money's another story. Priests don't hand out money, they take handouts. What do you think of priests? Do you like them?'

'Huh ... They're no different to anybody else.'

'Don't believe that for a second! Everyone else says no straight off. Priests say maybe, and that's the last you see of them.'

'Some of them are all right.'

'They're the worst!'

'Why's that?'

'Because they're the ones who give you hope, and there's nothing more dispiriting. Just around the corner, it's always just around the corner, heaven and all that jazz! It's one big hoax. Why not right now, huh? Why? Come on. They'll palm you off with some old rags even the abbé Pierre wouldn't be seen dead in. He gets given tons of them every day and he's never wearing them when you see him going on about Emmaus on TV. At your age, you should be wearing fashionable stuff. Come on, let's get something to eat. Stuff your face; everyone else is!'

Roland was in two minds. Although mildly disgusted by the chubby little hand resting on his knee, he had a feeling he would get more out of this one than the priest. When the latter returned with his three threadbare jumpers and a fifty-franc note, there was no one to be seen. The poor were not what they used to be.

Rodolphe dragged Roland to a bar in the marketplace where they consumed copious amounts of cheap charcuterie and white wine amid the butchers' stalls. By ten o'clock they were drunk. The blind man kept on and on talking while Roland gobbled up everything on his plate, nodding along at random points in the monologue. It was best to stay on the right side of mad people.

'Destiny, Roland, destiny! The wheel of fortune never stops turning and it's me giving it a push every morning when I open my dead eyes and see nothing. Place your bets, the chips are down!'

'Can I finish off the rillettes?'

After barging their way through the crowds, none of whom dared to say anything to the disabled man, they ended up in Monoprix where Roland was treated to a pair of jeans, a jumper and a bright-red down jacket. Next door at André he completed the outfit with a pair of walking shoes he had been eyeing up for months. He could feel the snow crunching under his grooved soles. He could have walked for days on end without getting tired. The sun was dusting the wide avenues with gold; the city looked fit for a king. In spite of the extreme cold, he felt on fire.

'You ever taken cocaine, Rodolphe?'

'No.'

'Well, it's just like this. You feel totally clean, brand new, invincible. Shit, when I think I almost pegged it last night ...'

'Destiny, Roland, it's destiny!'

They found themselves at the gates of the park leading to the Bassin de Neptune. Roland grabbed the bars with both hands. The kings lived on the other side of the fence.

'Can we go in? You don't have to pay to get in?'

'No.'

The frozen pond reflected the sky back at itself. Around its sides, statues draped in khaki-coloured tarpaulins revealed the occasional outstretched arm, a hint of knee, shoulder or buttock. In the middle of the mirror, Neptune and his chariot appeared set to take off for the heavens. Such beauty was painful to behold.

'You know what, Rodolphe? I could really do with some sunglasses, and also some gloves.'

'No problem. Is there a bench? I'd like to sit down.'

Good dog that he was, Roland led Rodolphe to a stone bench where he sat down, gasping for breath. Roland took the opportunity to run around, stomping the virgin snow under his heavy shoes, buzzing like a climber at the summit. He sent snowballs sliding over the icy surface of the pond, grenades of happiness exploding in the dazzling light.

Light ... Rodolphe could feel it but he couldn't see it. What was it like? A sound echoing on for ever? How could he know what anything was like? He had no points of reference. He could only touch the stone of the bench, the hard ground at the end of his stick, and touching was not enough. Others at the Institute for the Blind accepted the way they were, found compromises and positives in their situation … He never could. At the very beginning, he had been able to remember shapes, vague colours, light and dark, and then it had all gone. Just enough to make his mouth water before the plate was snatched from under his nose.

'Roland, I'm cold!'

In spite of Roland having assured him he wasn't hungry, Rodolphe insisted on going for lunch at the little restaurant next to the Théâtre Montansier.

'I swear, Rodolphe, after the amount we stuffed ourselves with this morning, I really don't need any more to eat.'

'Who cares? 'Tis the season to be wasteful.'

It was more of a liquid lunch; Rodolphe sent all the dishes back to the kitchen practically untouched, claiming they were either too hot or too cold. Roland didn't know where to put himself.

'You're going too far now. Why are you acting like such an arsehole?'

'Listen. The other day, I was waiting for the bus. It were chucking it down. I was standing on the edge of the gutter. I heard a lorry coming. Everybody behind me stepped back. Not one of them thought to take my arm. I was soaked to the skin. And you're asking me to like these people?'

They spent the afternoon at the Cyrano, which was showing *One Hundred and One Dalmatians*. The usher had to shake them, they were snoring so loudly.

Right from the first mouthful, the brandy had got the pump going again. The lava was flowing deliciously through his veins, spreading from his heart to the tips of his fingers and toes and into every follicle, even the tiniest nasal hair. Olivier felt as if he were coming home after a long, long time away. As the liquid in his glass went down, the molten metal pouring into him formed an internal suit of armour, making him a chrome-plated, invincible man of steel. His first drink and here, in front of him, his first love. Jesus, what had he been thinking, dying so early? He was just beginning to come back to life.

'Jeanne, do you remember the island?'

'Of course I do.'

The island was everywhere: under the dining-room table or the tree in the yard, in the patch behind Madame Stasi's corner shop, at the line B bus stop. They carried it with them wherever they went; they were the island, a mound of sand with a palm tree and Jeanne and Olivier standing under it like the model bride and groom on a wedding cake. There was no way to take them off it.

'I went there, you know. To Réunion, Mauritius … I missed you so much …'

'I went too, in books.'

'Do you still believe in it?'

'I've never stopped believing.'

Olivier poured himself a third glass. If he kept topping up the old furnace he would never be cold again. Three loud knocks shook the door.

'What's that?'

'I don't know.'

The knocking intensified. On the other side of the oak panel someone was bellowing.

'Jeanne! For fuck's sake, open up! I've forgotten my keys.'

Jeanne got up, letting out a sigh. It was as if a stone had smashed through the window.

'It's Rodolphe. Excuse me.'

Olivier sank deeper into the sofa. His iron armour had turned to lead. His feet felt huge, as if attached to a concrete plinth. From the hallway he could hear raised voices.

'Here she comes, about fucking time!'

'Stop shouting, I've got company.'

'So have I! Come on in, Roland. This is my sister, Jeanne.'

Olivier would have liked to sit up normally, perhaps with his legs casually crossed, but he could not do it. His muscles refused to obey him. Rodolphe entered the living room, snapping his white stick shut like a switchblade. He was scarlet, like a fat Chinese lantern. He staggered over to Olivier, holding out his hand.

'Hi, Rodolphe.'

Jeanne and a tall guy in a red jacket followed close behind him. Olivier managed to scramble to his feet.

'Evening, Olivier.'

'Olivier, as in olive tree? Well, why don't we call you apple tree or Christmas tree instead. 'Tis the season, after all!'

He fell back onto the sofa Olivier had just vacated, laughing heartily. His stick rolled under the sideboard.

'Rodolphe, please!'

The tall guy was shuffling his feet awkwardly in the doorway.

'Monsieur Christmas Tree! It's got a ring to it, hasn't it? How do you do, Monsieur Christmas Tree?'

The blind man's belly was shaking. The bulb hanging from the ceiling was reflected in his black glasses. He appeared to have lemur eyes. Suddenly he calmed down and his face turned serious.

'Sorry, I've had a bit to drink. You know how it is at this time of year, you let yourself go.'

'No harm done.'

'See, Jeanne! No harm done!'

Jeanne shrugged.

'Right then, let's not stand around. Make yourselves comfortable, everyone. Can I get you a drink, Monsieur …?'

'Toutin, Roland Toutin. I don't want to put you to any trouble. I was just bringing your brother home …'

'It's no trouble at all. Olivier?'

'Please.'

Rodolphe looked lost in thought. He had never known his sister to have people round. Only once, when one of her colleagues drove her home after her car broke down.

'Are you a colleague of Jeanne's?'

'Um, no. I'm the son of your neighbour who has just passed away.'

'And you're already on first-name terms?'

Jeanne stepped in, while handing out the glasses.

'We met a long time ago. Olivier is the brother of a friend of mine from boarding school.'

'Ah! A school friend ... Small world, isn't it?'

'We met again by chance. I came to borrow a phone book and—'

'By chance, that's right ...'

The ensuing silence made the room's already stuffy atmosphere even heavier. Olivier had the urge to rush at the window and fling it open.

'Your mother's name was Verdier?'

'That's right.'

'So you're Olivier Verdier?'

'You guessed it!'

Jeanne lit a cigarette. Rodolphe could not have been aware of what happened. He had been too little when it was covered up and no one had talked about it since. But she knew her brother and his talent for finding weak spots.

'Why don't you leave Olivier alone now, Rodolphe? He's come back to bury his mother. Can't you be a bit more sensitive?'

'You're right. Forgive me, Olivier, I can't help myself, I'm pathologically nosy. It must come from my disability; I always feel as though I'm missing out.'

'It's fine.'

Roland's hangover was already setting in. He felt as if he

had landed in the middle of a play without knowing his lines or even what role he was acting. He was torn between the urge to get back into the open air and the fear of losing the chance of a warm place to sleep. Rodolphe had promised to put him up for the night.

'Honestly, where are my manners? I haven't introduced you to Roland. We met this morning in God's house, at Notre-Dame.'

'What the hell were you doing there?'

'Confessing, Jeanne, confessing, seeking forgiveness for having hurt you last night. Either that or I had to pee. Whatever, one way or the other I had a pressing need to go inside. Roland is ... "without fixed abode", that's the expression, isn't it? He was waiting for the idiot priest to dole out some old clothes and a few francs. Not likely! You know what a big softie I am and everything ... Anyway, we had a brilliant day together. He's going to sleep at my place tonight.'

'Suit yourself.'

'Thanks, Jeanne. Ooh, now here's an idea! Four lonely hearts: why don't we all have supper together?'

Olivier had not phoned Odile, or the lawyer, still less Emmaus. He had forgotten. He had decided to forget everything, and the rest. It gave him a pleasure akin to that of a child skipping school. Ever since his treatment two years ago, he had got into the habit of writing a list of everything he had to do the next day, and derived a slavish satisfaction from seeing it through to the end. This now seemed like the stupidest thing imaginable. He had failed to complete a single one of today's tasks and would put his mind to keeping up the same record tomorrow. Rid of the burden of his chores, he felt lighter, freer. Tomorrow was the perfect cupboard in which to shelve what had not been done today. The medals awarded to good little recovered alcoholics seemed to him to be made of the same chocolate as the ones they gave to the war wounded, whichever war it was this time. To hell with them, to hell with the lot of them. He no longer had any wish to be prim and proper, to set a good example, to be praised for his hard work. He had done enough hard work. Now he just wanted to enjoy life, to take advantage of things that normally passed him by. The jack-in-the-box had sprung out, the genie had emerged from its bottle. Of course there would be a price to pay; what did it matter? What was the point of scrimping and saving? So what if his mother had died in the bed he was now stretched out on? Dead people were toothless; there was nothing she could do to stop him. She was cold, frozen stiff like a breaded fish fillet. He, on the other hand, was burning with fever, like Jeanne across the hall. He had been building up to this moment for years. No one could take it away from him. It had been a long, painful slog, but he had walked that road, searched for the Holy Grail and he had found her again; they still loved one another, it was still the same …

Olivier hauled himself up by holding on to the side of the bed. He weighed a ton! Emotion, that was it, all the emotion. He had one last drop of Negrita, just a drop. The Negress on the label gave him a wink.

'None of that, love, I'm spoken for!'

He put his hand over his mouth and exhaled. The problem with rum was that it stank something awful.

He would go out and buy a bottle of champagne and tell them in the shop he had just had a rum toddy for a cold. It would hardly be surprising, in this weather. Actually, you know what, fuck it, he had nothing to apologise for, he wouldn't say anything to anyone. His key, where had he put his key? The flat was all lopsided, it was impossible to tell the floor from the ceiling. It was dark everywhere, narrow, gut-red … his key, damn it!

He knocked over a frame, which fell and broke. It was a picture of himself with his hair brushed to one side and his arms crossed, a school photo. He slid down the wall, ignoring the blood on his finger.

'What are you looking at me like that for, huh? She's back; *Mathilde est revenue!*'

He seemed to hear the kid in the photo reply, 'You poor old thing, you poor old thing …'

He dropped the picture and reached the bathroom just in time to vomit all that was left of himself.

Jeanne was peeling potatoes and tucking them into a tin around a pallid chicken dotted with curls of butter. Rodolphe was sitting on the other side of the kitchen table, his eyes directed towards the ceiling. He was rolling pea-sized balls of soft bread between his fingers and lining them up on the oilcloth. The scene looked every inch the domestic idyll, a cosy snapshot of everyday life.

'What do you make of Roland?'

'I don't know. I've only just met him. Shy?'

'Yes, he is. He's young and hasn't had much luck in life. It's terrible being unlucky. There's no way of treating it, it's incurable; people avoid you like the plague. Take me, for example, even without my eyes, I'm better off than him. I've got a roof over my head, I can eat what I want when I want, and above all I have a sister to look out for me. He, on the other hand, has nothing, nothing but his unlucky self. Imagine that for company!'

'He had a stroke of luck today, meeting you.'

'That wasn't luck. He's part of a carefully crafted plan.'

'Planned by you?'

'Oh, no! I'm just a humble cog in the magnificent machine.'

'Well, for the time being, he's got a warm bed for the night and a roast chicken dinner.'

Jeanne stood up, wiped her hands on her apron and pushed back a strand of hair that had fallen in front of her eyes. She looked like a person with a song in her head, a little tune with a calming effect. As she opened the oven door to slide in the tin, a puff of hot air engulfed the small kitchen. Rodolphe jumped.

'The breath of hell! So you don't believe a word of it?'

'A word of what? Hell?'

'No! The plan, the cogs, all the jigsaw pieces slotting into place. You think it's all perfectly normal, this reunion with Olivier?'

Even though Rodolphe could not see the blood rising in her face, Jeanne turned away and ran her hands under the tap.

'Aren't you going to answer me?'

'What do you want me to say? It's chance, it's life, it's really not that unusual. A friend's brother who—'

'What kind of idiot do you take me for? Do you think I don't know your little story?'

Jeanne turned off the tap and gripped the edge of the sink.

'Jeanne Mangin and Olivier Verdier, aged fifteen and sixteen respectively, suspected of the kidnap and murder of two-year-old Luc Flamand, for whom Jeanne babysat. Hastily drawn-up ransom note, five days of anguish for the parents ending in the discovery of the little body in Fausses-Reposes forest. Of course, it was never proven, and it was a poor unfortunate tramp who got the blame because the Mangins had friends in the right places and something had to be done to put an end to the whole business ...'

'Shut up!'

Using the flat of his hand, Rodolphe swept the dozen little bread balls off the table, sending them scattering and bouncing on the chequered tile floor. It was no longer a little ditty going round in Jeanne's head, but the blades of a helicopter whipping up the black clouds of an impending storm.

'I don't give a fuck whether you killed the kid or not, whether the tramp was innocent or not, what sticks in my mind is "Jeanne and Olivier", like "Romeo and Juliet" or "Héloïse and Abélard". Your little love affair was all anyone talked about, cooing over "the little married couple"! Since nursery school! The whole world revolved around you. They put you on a pedestal, so well-behaved, so polite, so perfect, so revoltingly self-obsessed. As for me, I had no eyes, I held out my hand to you and when you didn't take it, I strained my ears instead, and I heard everything!'

Jeanne had let go of the sink and sat back down at the table. Her legs no longer held her. She placed her hands flat against the oilcloth and closed her eyes. The black space inside her head was being bombarded with phosphorescent images from long ago: a pram, a cabin in the woods, a postcard of an island covered in palm trees, letters cut out of a newspaper, a pillow so soft and malleable you would never believe it capable of killing ...

'He's back, Jeanne, he's back!'

'It was an accident. Just an accident. We wanted to leave ...'

Rodolphe didn't recognise his sister's voice. It quivered like the voice of an old lady or a little girl.

'I said, I don't care! You could have killed half the human race and I still wouldn't give a shit. Just tell me you don't feel anything for him, that it's all over, finished!'

Little by little, something inside her was righting itself, like those Chinese paper flowers which blossom on contact with water, the first tears shed in so long. Her heart was opening up. At the same time, she was becoming aware of the danger her brother's distress represented. Rodolphe was not the kind of kid you could smother with a pillow. She took three deep breaths.

The scent of roast chicken was beginning to fill the air, a reassuring smell.

'Of course it's over. I'm sorry ... Do you remember that line of Lacenaire in *Les Enfants du Paradis*? "The past that leaps at your face like a rabid cat." He's leaving anyway, in three or four days, after his mother's funeral. He's married, he lives on the Côte d'Azur. It's all so far behind us!'

Rodolphe didn't reply. He had gone back to fashioning little balls of bread, keeping an ear on his sister as she opened the fridge, took out a lettuce and began separating the leaves, sniffling as she went.

Liar, filthy fucking liar ...

Hangovers always had the lingering aftertaste of a funfair: lurid wooden horses dancing a merry-go-round inside the head, a sugar-coated palate and tongue, a whiff of stale fat in the nostrils and fluorescent confetti floating before the eyes. Lying tangled in bed sheets steeped in the sour tang of sweat, Olivier felt as if he had been plaited into a rope of marshmallow. He could not even find the strength to hang up, leaving the receiver dangling on the cord and emitting a monotonous beep.

Odile had found the number on the Minitel. She had been trying to get through until one o'clock the night before. Where had he been? Why had he not called? Why had he started drinking again? Why? Why? Each 'why' resounded in his head like the blow of a sledgehammer.

'I dunno, I dunno,' was all he managed to say in reply. Eventually he mustered the energy to start explaining about the transport problems brought on by the bad weather, but she already knew about them.

'I know, darling, I heard it on the news. It's unbelievable in this day and age. Maybe that's why you ... you let yourself go. And besides I'm sure your mother's death has hit you more than you care to admit. Even if you weren't on the best of terms, she was still your mum. All the memories must be coming back ... I understand, my love, but you need to look after yourself. You need to be strong ...'

He let her build up a list of excuses he could never have come up with by himself and then she rang off, promising to call again that evening and sending love and strength at this difficult time.

It was still dark outside. The chrome lamp in the shape of a giant sprig of lily of the valley lit only one corner of the bedside table and a patch of the rug, which was decorated with swarms of red and green arabesques. Olivier closed his eyes again. For a moment he pictured Odile, immaculately coiffed and made up, emerging from Résidence des Mimosas at the wheel of her black Polo, jumping the stop sign she considered unnecessary before weaving her way through the traffic to reach the shop, where Mireille would be pacing up and down. In a lull between permed customers, Odile would tell her everything.

How far away she seemed – and not just geographically.

All he had retained of the previous day's events was a collection of jumbled, fragmented images in no particular order: Rodolphe circling the table with the camcorder clamped to his dead eye like a monstrous prosthesis, indiscriminately filming the dinner, the ceiling, faces, a spoon falling off the table; Roland perching stiffly on the edge of his seat, constantly offering to wash up before the meal was even over; Jeanne, ghostly pale, chain-smoking cigarettes; and himself chain-drinking without even checking what was in the glass – champagne, wine, brandy, more wine. The room was immersed in gloom like a murky fish tank, with a shiny glint of cutlery or crystal here and there. It was bizarre, extraordinary, and yet Olivier felt as if he was attending a family reunion, *his own* family reunion. Rodolphe had even called him 'my brother-in-law' several times, until his sister told him to pack it in.

'What? We all know how it is with friends' brothers …! Anyway, it's all water under the bridge now, isn't it? Done and dusted, wiped clean, swept under the carpet …'

It was always hard to tell what Rodolphe was playing at. There were two sides to him: refined one minute and coarse the next. Light and shadow alternated on his moon-shaped face.

To tell the truth, Olivier didn't care what Rodolphe was up

to. The alcohol had numbed him; he was untouchable. Rodolphe was just a bit-part in this scene, like Roland, who was rushing to clear the table. Olivier only had eyes for Jeanne. He discovered her anew with every little gesture: the way she pushed a stray lock of hair from her forehead or rubbed her nose before snapping at her brother, how she rested her chin in the palm of her hand and glanced at him sidelong. Their gazes would meet in a kind of electric arc, a bridge leading from one to the other. At that moment, everything around them became a blur, all of life's sounds, words and cries dissolved to nothing and the island, their island, emerged once more. Their lashes stopped blinking, their pupils dilated, they feasted on the sight of one another until tears filled their eyes. Several times at nursery school the teacher had panicked and been forced to shake them out of their growing state of catalepsy. 'Stop that at once! Look at them, their eyes are all red!'

From that age, long before they were able to put it into words, they had sworn to one another they would never leave the island.

Olivier didn't react until the third ring. He had heard the bell the first two times, but failed to connect it with himself. He almost broke his neck taking his first step out of bed. His foot had landed on an empty bottle of Negrita which was now rolling across the parquet floor, alternately revealing and concealing the dazzling grin of the West Indian woman in her headscarf.

The bell rang again. It was as if it were directly wired to his nervous system.

'Coming!'

The clothes he had slept in clung to his skin. Madeleine glared at him with her little porcelain eyes, bundled up to her weaselly nose in her frayed black astrakhan coat, her scarf wrapped three times around her vulturous neck, a shapeless brown woolly hat on her head and spindly legs planted in red fur-lined boots that looked like flower pots.

'Is this a bad time?'

'Um … no. What did you … ?'

She stepped back in disgust, catching a whiff of his foul breath.

'Are you ill? You don't look very well. Oh, don't you worry, I know exactly how you feel, you poor thing. So anyway, I've come about the wreath.'

'The what?'

'The wreath, the flowers for your poor maman! Would you like me to take care of it? I'm going into town anyway and I thought to myself maybe you wouldn't be up to …'

'The wreath … Yes, of course, if you want to, Madeleine.'

'Great, leave it to me. I've got very good taste, and I'm a dab hand at this sort of thing. If you only knew how many I've seen go before me! What do you want written on it?'

'Written on what?'

'On the wreath! "To my dear maman" … "To my mother"? You need to choose something. I'm going to put: "To my neighbour, sadly missed." It's simple, but it gets the message across. I'll pick up a pot plant, even though nothing will survive in this weather. Well then?'

It was freezing out on the landing. Olivier rubbed his bare feet together and wrapped his arms around himself, hands tucked under his armpits.

'Whatever you think, Madeleine. You know better than I do about these things.'

'OK, well then, I'll put: "To my mother, from her loving son". That's got quite a nice ring to it, hasn't it?'

'Very nice, yes. I'm sure you'll do a great job, Madeleine. Goodbye, thank you.'

He was about to close the door, but the old woman edged closer.

'It's just … about paying for it …'

'Oh, yes, sorry. I'll sign a cheque and you can write in the amount.'

'You can trust me. I'll give you the receipt!'

The sound of Madeleine's voice was like a fork scraping against a dish. He went back inside the flat to look for his jacket. He eventually found it scrunched up in a corner, and took out the cheque book. The old woman had not moved an inch. She was like a statue, the doormat her plinth.

'Do you have a pen?'

'No, I don't, I'm afraid.'

'Right, OK, well, how about you pay for it and I'll pay you back later. Sorry, I'm coming down with a rotten cold; I think I might be ill already.'

'OK then. Is there a maximum you want to spend?'

'I don't know, Madeleine, whatever you think. See you later, thank you.'

He slammed the door in her face and slumped back against it. He was dripping with sweat. It was streaming down his back, zigzagging across his forehead. His stomach was seized with a sudden need to vomit. He gulped back his saliva and took several deep breaths. 'Calm down, no need to panic. You just overdid it a bit last night. You'll get over it, everything's fine.' He incanted these magic words over and over and by the time he got back to sprawl on his bed, he felt much better.

The distorted reflection of his face in the back of a teaspoon. That was the only image he remembered from the end of the dinner party. Rodolphe had kept topping him up as if trying to drown him, which he succeeded in doing. Jeanne had disappeared, leaving the three men to ramble on around the wreckage of the meal. Roland was giggling for no apparent reason while watching Rodolphe film the dregs on plates, in glasses and at the bottom of wine bottles. 'The dregs of the dregs!' as he called them. And then there was him, Olivier, leaning on the table gazing at his own reflection in the convex mirror of a teaspoon. Afterwards? Total blackout. He was now kicking himself. How could he have let himself get into that state when he had Jeanne right there in front of him and should have grabbed her by the hand and taken her away, somewhere far from this seedy, sleazy atmosphere. Alcohol. It was down to the alcohol and Rodolphe, who had immediately identified Olivier's weak spot. He was disgusted with himself. He felt like banging his head against the wall. He had just been reunited with his one true love and the best he could offer her was the pitiful sight of a raving alcoholic. All things considered, maybe it was better this way. The past was history and they had their own lives to go back to. The emotion of seeing her again had gone to his head. So many years had passed, they were not the people they once were. Those versions of themselves were dead and buried.

Was Jeanne still Jeanne? Why should life, which spares no one, make an exception for her? The same thing happened every time he drank: he found himself spinning the tiniest incident into an epic novel. No doubt it was because his life was made up of a chain of banal events. The fact of the matter was the island had been submerged. He was now cut off from the beautiful story he preserved in a corner of his heart the way grandmothers keep their wedding tiaras in glass domes. Fate had intervened to take away his one pure place of refuge. He should never have come back to this shithole. Dirty, the whole place was dirty and old, even the daylight beginning to filter through the curtains. He had to do something to lift his mood, take a shower, for example. He threw off the covers, leapt out of bed and charged into the bathroom.

Roland was kneeling on the tiled floor with his feet turned in and his head and arms dangling into the bathtub, from which an appalling stench of sick was rising.

'Shit! What the fuck's *he* doing here?'

Olivier covered his nose with one hand and shook Roland with the other. The moron wasn't moving.

'Roland! Shit, Roland, wake up!'

Still nothing. Olivier grabbed Roland under the arms and pulled him backwards. He screamed and dropped him when he saw his face.

Roland's skin was tinged purple, an enormous black tongue lolled between his blue lips and his glassy eyes were bulging out of his head. Olivier's tie was knotted tightly around his neck.

'No, this isn't happening … it can't be.'

Olivier sprang out of the bathroom. He roamed the flat – for how long, he did not know – with his hands clamped over his mouth and his mind blazing, incapable of the slightest coherent thought. He was like a trapped bird flapping wildly around a room.

He flung the kitchen window open and received a blast of icy morning air. He closed his eyes and waited for his mind to settle. Even though he knew he had not been hallucinating, he went back to the bathroom to check, peering in from the doorway, too afraid to go in. Roland was still there, his nightmarish head wedged between the bidet and the base of the sink, arms and legs splayed swastika-like, just as Olivier had left him.

'What happened? What the hell happened?'

No matter how hard he racked his brains, his memory stayed blank; he could not even remember how he had got home. Back when he was an alcoholic, he had often experienced blackouts, sometimes wiping out entire days. He had no idea where he had been or what he had done. People would tell him, 'I saw you in such and such a place last night; you were wasted!' and he would go along with it without having a clue what they were referring to. It was quite frightening. He had always worried he might do something really stupid while he was out of it. And now ... No, he couldn't have! Besides, what reason could he have had for killing the poor sod? There was none, they had got on perfectly well ... But alcohol has its own reasons, which reason doesn't come into. What should he do, call the police? It was more than he could manage. Whom could he turn to? Odile?

He went back into the bedroom and sat on the edge of the bed with his head in his hands, staring at the telephone. 'Hello, Odile. Guess what? When I got out of bed this morning I found a guy lying dead in the bathroom with my tie around his neck. It might have been me who strangled him, I have no idea.' It was impossible. They were no longer living on the same planet. Jeanne, then. It had to be Jeanne. He could hardly believe the way the past was boomeranging back to him: they would be partners in crime again. The rusty old machine was cranking back to life, squeaking inside his head like the wheel of little Luc's pram. Not only had he let her down with his shocking behaviour the previous night, now he was contemplating dragging her into a sordid murder. He couldn't do it to her. But he couldn't just sit here either. He felt incapable of making the slightest decision. He needed advice, someone to tell him what to do or at least point him in the right direction.

He got dressed, shaking all over. It took forever to button up his shirt and even longer to find his keys, which he finally located in his jacket pocket. His hand hovered over the buzzer for a long time before he pressed it. It felt like sticking a finger into an electric socket. His heart sank when Rodolphe's voice came back through the door asking, 'Who is it?'

'Um ... Olivier.'

He heard a bolt being slid back and then the door opened.

Rodolphe was wearing a garnet-red Pyrenean-wool dressing gown and tartan carpet slippers. He seemed in buoyant mood.

'Come in, come in, Olivier. Not too much the worse for wear? You hit it hard last night!'

'I'm sorry, I ...'

'Ah, don't be silly, we've all been there. Come on in – the coffee's still warm, it'll do you good.'

There was no trace of the previous night's battleground on the table; it had all been swept away, scrubbed clean, as if nothing had happened. The room was filled with an aroma of fresh coffee and toast that could make you believe in the possibility of contentment.

'Take a seat. I'll get you a bowl.'

Unconsciously, Olivier chose the same place he had occupied the night before, as though trying to take the scene from the top and play it differently this time. Rodolphe returned from the kitchen and set a steaming bowl of coffee down in front of him. Olivier took a sip and almost choked when the blind man asked, 'Is Roland not up yet?'

'I ... I don't know.'

'He didn't sleep in his room so I guessed he must have crashed at yours. You left together last night – don't you remember?'

'Um ...'

'Well, you did! You started having a go at him at one point. I can't remember what it was about ... Oh, yes! You told him he didn't know what love was after he'd made some smutty comment about women. You made up a while later and seeing as we'd finished all the wine, you asked everyone back to yours for a nightcap. Personally, I'd had enough, so I didn't come. I like a drink too, but as soon as I hit a red light, that's it! Off goes the engine.'

Olivier's head was filled with a thick liquid which sloshed

from side to side like the contents of a shaken jar. The smell of coffee was making him queasy.

'Something's wrong, isn't it, Olivier? I can tell ... Oh, I know what it is! He's gone, hasn't he? He's stolen your wallet and done a runner. The little bastard! You can't trust these people. Only ... it's weird he left his jacket and bag behind. They were on his bed when I went into his room this morning ...'

Without his dark glasses on, Rodolphe's cross-eyed gaze was directed towards a point just above Olivier's head. He was slowly running his fingertips over the oilcloth, pleating the edges between his fingers. Olivier was on the verge of going crazy. He leapt to his feet, knocking over his chair.

'No, dammit! It's not that ... Where's Jeanne?'

'She's gone shopping. What's the matter, Olivier? Calm down! How about a drink? I managed to save a bottle of brandy from last night's carnage. It's a good one; it would have been a waste. It'll perk you up. Have a seat in the armchair and tell me what's up.'

Olivier slumped into the chair with his head in his hands and his elbows on his knees. Rodolphe may not have been the person he was hoping to confide in, but better this than be left alone with his thoughts.

'There you go. Get that down you.'

Olivier downed the brandy in one. A rush of warmth ran from his head to his feet and the tremors racking his body abruptly ceased. Rodolphe poured him another glass, which he drained in the same way as the first. He was starting to breathe almost normally. He sat back and closed his eyes, arms dangling either side of the chair.

'He's dead.'

'What are you talking about?'

'He's in the bathroom, dead.'

'Dead how?'

'Strangled.'

'What! You mean hanged? Is that it, he's hanged himself in the bathroom? Committed suicide?'

'I don't know, I don't know anything about it! I found him slumped against the bathtub this morning with sick everywhere and my tie round his neck. I can't remember any of it! This is a nightmare!'

A wave swept over him. Olivier curled up, tears streaming over his hands, his back heaving with sobs. Rodolphe pulled up a chair alongside him, holding the brandy bottle in his hands. He had put his black glasses on and kept repeating, 'With your tie … with your tie …' until they heard a key in the door.

Jeanne appeared holding a basket with a bunch of leeks sticking out of it, emanating a haze of chill carried in from outside. Olivier kept his head down.

'What's going on here? Rodolphe?'

'It seems our friend here has a problem. A very big problem.'

Jeanne put her basket on the table, took off her coat and knelt down in front of Olivier.

'Olivier? … What is it? Is something wrong? … Olivier, answer me.'

Olivier went on hiding his face and shaking his head. He didn't want her to see him like this. Besides, even if he tried to speak, no words would come out, as his Adam's apple appeared to have swollen to the size of a pétanque ball.

'Rodolphe, what's happened? Tell me!'

'When he woke up this morning, he found Roland dead in his bathroom, strangled with his tie.'

'What are you talking about? What do you— ?'

'Calm down, Jeanne, I'm only repeating what he's just told me. The two of them left here last night pretty well pissed and went across the hall for one final drink. That's the last thing he remembers. Total blackout.'

Jeanne stood up and took a few steps over to the window, parting the curtain slightly. It had snowed during the night but the road was already dirty, covered in crossings-out. She slowly made her way back across the room, sat on the arm of Olivier's chair and wrapped her arm around his shoulders.

'Is it true, Olivier? Is that what happened?'

With his hand covering his mouth, he lifted his head and nodded. His eyes and nose were streaming. The hair slicked to his forehead made him look as if he had been pulled from the sea.

'Can you really not remember anything?'

'No, nothing. I don't understand ...'

He didn't recognise the sound of his own voice. It was breaking like that of an adolescent, veering from low to high from one syllable to the next. Rodolphe poured himself a brandy and cleared his throat.

'Maybe he hanged himself and the tie came unhooked. We should go and have a look.'

'No! I don't want to go back there!'

Olivier's hand gripped Jeanne's knee beside him on the armrest.

'Rodolphe's right, Olivier. That's bound to be what happened. The guy was clearly at the end of his rope. He must have been feeling low after a few drinks ... And anyway, why on earth would you have killed him? It's ridiculous!'

Olivier was slowly coming round to this idea. It made sense. The mental blackout had made him panic. Roland had killed himself; that was the only possible explanation. A glimmer of hope had sprung from the depths of the abyss. He wiped his face with the back of his sleeve, sniffing.

'OK, let's go over there. Rodolphe, can I have another glass?'

As they went deeper into the flat, the smell of vomit intensified until, approaching the bathroom, it became unbearable. Olivier pushed open the door but could not stand to look.

'Oh my God!'

Jeanne froze in the doorway, her shoulders shuddering as she retched. Then she took a step inside. She struggled to turn her eyes from Roland's broken-doll body in order to study the ceiling. There was nothing remotely like a hook, not even a light fitting. The room's only illumination was provided by a strip light on the wall above the cabinet. The two ends of the tie were hanging either side of the neck, and there was no slipknot to be seen. Hovering just outside the door, Rodolphe was becoming agitated.

'What can you see, Jeanne?'

'Nothing. Nothing that helps. Olivier, was he like this when you found him?'

'No, he was kneeling against the bath with his head and arms dangling into the tub.'

'Did you undo the tie?'

'No, I didn't touch anything. I thought he was asleep so I pulled him backwards. I let go when I realised he was dead.'

Jeanne scoured the walls for clues that might back up the theory of suicide, but she drew a blank. Rodolphe kept pressing her.

'Are you sure there's nothing on the ceiling?'

'I told you, there's nothing there!'

'Well then, he can't have hanged himself.'

Olivier went back out into the corridor, threw himself against the wall and slid to the floor. The tiny flicker of hope had been extinguished. Clenching his jaw, he muttered, 'It wasn't me! It wasn't me!' but even he was not convinced. He would almost prefer to have killed the man and remember doing it than not know either way. He could slap himself as many times as he liked, nothing was coming back to him. Jeanne and Rodolphe were trying to calm him down when two rings at the door made all three of them freeze.

'Shit! It's Madeleine ... I can't, I can't!'

'You have to, Olivier. Tell her you're ill, make her go away, but you must answer the door.'

His legs could barely hold him. They seemed to be working independently of one another and he could not get them to move in sync. The door seemed to be miles away. The little old lady looked even more wizened than she had done that morning.

'Ah, you're in, jolly good. Oh, but I must say you're not looking any better! Would you like me to call a doctor?'

'No, thank you, Madeleine. I've taken an aspirin. I just need to keep warm.'

'Suit yourself, but you must be careful in this deathly cold. Personally, I get the flu jab at the first sign of winter. If you like, I could warm up some broth for you. I've got some left over from—'

'No, I'll be fine.'

'OK, OK. Right then, I did as we discussed, I've got a lovely wreath with the message "To my dear maman". It's more affectionate, don't you think? I picked up a chrysanthemum to give from me, just the one but it's a good size and—'

'I'm sorry, but I'm very tired. How much do I owe you?'

'Yes, yes, I understand. Here's the receipt then ... They had cheaper ones, but for your maman ...'

'Just a second, I'll write you a cheque.'

Olivier was filling in the amount when he heard Madeleine entering the flat.

'Goodness, there's a funny smell in here ...'

'Don't come in! I've been sick and I haven't had a chance to clean up. Here's your cheque, thanks again, goodbye.'

Before the old woman could draw breath, Olivier had closed the door on her. He heard her muttering to herself before hobbling off down the stairs. Hundreds of tiny stars were dancing before his eyes. He was thirsty.

Times like these called for leek soup. In fact, perhaps making soup was the best thing to do. Olivier's snores travelled from the armchair where he was slumped in the lounge to the kitchen where Jeanne was peeling vegetables. The alcohol and sleeping pills had finally overcome his nerves. Rodolphe had gone for a walk around the block, calm was restored and she felt at home again.

After leaving the flat opposite, Olivier had gone through every stage of hysteria, from absolute dejection, convinced his only option was suicide, to almost mystical bursts of elation which made him want to run naked through the streets, banging his fists against his chest, blaming himself for all the wrong in the world and briefly hearing the voice of reason telling him to hand himself in at the nearest police station. Only after the two Mogadon pills had kicked in could a more pragmatic solution be considered. With Olivier out for the count, Rodolphe had stretched out his limbs and sighed.

'Well, here we go again!'

'What?'

'The two of you, with the body of an innocent victim on your hands. Correct me if I'm wrong, but I don't suppose you're planning on calling the emergency services, are you?'

'No more than you are.'

'Ah, but it would suit me just fine to see the back of that arsehole. One quick phone call and it's timber for Olivier the olive tree!'

'You wouldn't do it.'

'And why not?'

'Because you love playing the game, and it's not over yet. And because there's nothing to say you didn't go with them last night or decide to join them later.'

'Ah, come on! Have pity on a poor blind man! Would you really point the finger at your own brother? Anyway, what makes you so sure you'd escape the blame?'

'I'm not pointing the finger at anyone. I don't care who did it. The police, on the other hand ... You're the one who brought the guy home. People will have seen you together all around town.'

'So what? It's not my flat he died in.'

'No, the one directly opposite. Give it a rest. I know exactly where you're trying to go with this, and you can stop it now.'

'Fine. So what do you suggest? Fausses-Reposes forest?'

Jeanne had gone back to the flat. She had a hell of a job getting Roland's already stiffened limbs to lie straight against his body. It was like grappling with a partially defrosted chicken. Then she got on with cleaning the bathroom. Later on, when it was dark and Olivier had woken up, they would take the body down to the car and dump it in the woods. Just another settling of scores between rough-sleepers ...

Jeanne undid her apron. The pressure-cooker valve was beginning to whisper, puffing out steam which condensed in fine droplets on the dirty windowpanes. It smelt good, like sweat after making love. She and Olivier had only done it once, in the cabin deep in the woods. It was in August when everyone was away on holiday. They had made love because it needed to be done, like getting a passport or a vaccination. They were both virgins. Nature had done its best to help things along. It wasn't good or bad; they didn't know what it was. The air was heavy. Pulling their underwear back on afterwards, they felt damp, sticky and strangely sad. Later, when they brought little Luc there, they recognised the small brown bloodstain on the makeshift sofa, formed of the back seat of a Peugeot 203. It looked like an official seal.

From the moment she opened the door to Olivier, she had known for certain their destinies would be entwined again. It was like opening a book on the page it had been left at the night before. They had been asleep for twenty-five years and now they were waking up again, side by side, the stuff of fairy tales. Never mind that he had aged, that he was an alcoholic; their real life had always gone on in parallel to the life other people led. They had their own ways, their own language which made them constant. This deep conviction gave rise to a quiet strength that nothing in the world could undermine.

The valve began to whistle loudly: the soup was ready.

'I don't know, I don't know …'

Olivier was stirring his spoon around the bowl like a child reluctant to eat his soup.

'You should listen to Jeanne, Olivier. She's right, there's no risk of getting caught.'

'But a man's dead, for God's sake!'

'Yes and what about your life? Do you really want to throw it away because of one stupid mistake? Dozens of people like Roland die every day of cold or hunger or in fights, and no one even bothers to write about it. Anyway, trust me, Roland didn't give a shit about life.'

Olivier didn't know what to think. His brain was still dulled by booze and Mogadon pills. Jeanne had laid out her plan with disconcerting matter-of-factness. He had sat listening open-mouthed, as if she was telling him about the last film she had seen. It seemed crazy to him, utterly crazy. He had reached that stage of hangover between delirium and lucidity when the guilt and shame set in and you feel torn in every direction, all roads leading to disaster. One glass, just one glass of the Scotch Rodolphe had brought home with him and he would be able to make a decision.

'But, Jeanne, have you really thought about what I'm dragging you into?'

'What about you? Have you thought about what you'll drag me into if you don't accept my help? This is no one's fault, Olivier. No one's to blame.'

Rodolphe got up from the table and placed the bottle of Scotch in front of Olivier.

'Shall I pour you a glass?'

Around one in the morning, the bottle was almost empty and Olivier's bowl remained untouched, the soup long cold. For the last hour he had been checking his watch every five minutes.

'Shall we go then? Can we go now?'

Jeanne replied calmly that it was still too early and there was a chance they might pass someone on the stairs. Liberated by having made a decision, Olivier was no longer afraid of anything. How could he have considered handing himself in? Even if he had strangled Roland, it was only an accident or rather, as Rodolphe had explained, he had merely been the instrument of destiny, of Roland's destiny, which was always going to play out the same way. He wouldn't go so far as to say he had done him a favour, but it was getting there. And then there was Jeanne, who had come running the moment he needed her, ready to do whatever it took, just like the old days. He was ashamed he had ever doubted her. It was not just a coincidence; not for nothing were they being brought together again under such similar circumstances. There was another way to look at things than the nice ordered way we were taught. One day, a long time ago, he had sold out, given in, put on the starchy suit he had been handed, and that was why he started drinking, to cauterise this ugly wound. Tonight, he could have drunk enough to float an ocean liner and he still wouldn't feel pissed. His head was perfectly clear.

Jeanne stood up and glanced out of the window. There was no one around. As luck would have it, she had found a space to park her car right outside the building.

'I think we can go. How do you feel?'

'Fine, absolutely fine. I'm ready.'

Jeanne shook her brother, who was dozing with his hands resting on his stomach and his legs outstretched.

'Rodolphe, we're going.'

'Huh? Oh, right, yes. I'll send you a signal if I hear anything on the stairs.'

There was no longer anything frightening about Roland's body. It was just a cumbersome object that Jeanne and Olivier were wrapping up and tying inside a rug. A great big Christmas present. The telephone began to ring as they were heading out of the door. Jeanne and Olivier looked at one another, each bending over and holding one end of the rug. For a fraction of a second Olivier pictured Odile in her nightdress, biting her thumbnail in the pink light of the bedside lamp. It was such a bizarre image that he had to hold back a laugh.

'Is that your wife?'

He nodded.

'Let's go. On three.'

Rodolphe was waiting for them on the landing, warmly wrapped up and with a ridiculous red woolly hat on his head.

'Are you coming with us?'

'Of course! Who wouldn't trust a blind person?'

The telephone was still ringing when they reached the floor below.

The pushchair was rattling along the dusty path, the front right wheel squeaking as it turned. It was Jeanne pushing it, humming a tune that made little Luc laugh. Olivier was walking ahead carrying a rucksack. Inside there was enough baby food, milk and nappies to last several days. Tucked in his breast pocket, the ransom letter was burning against his chest like a poultice. His parents had gone away for a few days to stay with friends in the country. He had had to fight hard to be allowed to stay behind. He was sixteen, almost seventeen, and perfectly capable of being left home alone. He clinched it with a promise to call them every day.

Later, when Jeanne left him alone with Luc in the cabin, the die would be cast. She would return with the empty pushchair, telling them she had nodded off and woken to find him gone. The following day, the parents would receive the anonymous letter. She would come back to the cabin once a day while he went off to call his parents, until he picked up the money. At that point they would leave Luc at an agreed location and disappear, never to be seen again. It was the price they had to pay to reach the island. It was hot, as hot then as it was bitterly cold tonight.

Every detail of that day came back to Olivier as he waded up to his ankles through crisp snow. He could not see Jeanne but heard her breathing behind him. The woods became denser the further in they went. The branches snatched at their clothes and scratched their cheeks and hands. They fell over several times. Breathless, they came to a halt beside a place where the earth dipped into a kind of ditch.

'Here?'

'Yes, we've come far enough.'

They cut the ropes securing the rug and rolled the body into the bottom of the hole before covering it in twigs, dry leaves, and snow. It was falling again now. The heavens were smiling on them; tomorrow there would be no trace of their steps. They gathered up the ropes and rug and went back the way they had come. They took a couple of wrong turns but eventually made it back to the car in which Rodolphe was waiting for them, frozen rigid.

'You took your time!'

On the contrary, to Jeanne and Olivier it all seemed to have happened in the space of five minutes. Jeanne started the car and moved off slowly. The snowflakes were soundlessly pelting the windscreen, swept away immediately by the wipers. Olivier remembered that when he was little, he always used to volunteer to wipe the blackboard at school. He loved it. He was reliving that pleasure tonight. Everything was clean and tidy, the satisfaction of a job done. All mistakes had been erased, they could start anew.

Back at home, Rodolphe had to face facts: he was the third wheel. The other two were united in silence, forcing him to retreat into himself. His quips, bad puns and snide remarks were like water off a duck's back. He swiped the remaining Scotch before Olivier had a chance to pour himself a glass, and went and shut himself in his room. It was a petty thing to do, and made him feel no better. In fact, far from having the desired effect of knocking him out, the alcohol wound him up even further. He could not sleep. He tossed and turned under the duvet like a boar in its wallow. Too hot, too cold. They were bound to have sex. No doubt about it, the bastard was going to fuck his sister. He, whose knowledge of sex was limited to the subtle pleasures of the occasional quickie with a whore or, more frequently, with his right hand, refused to think of Jeanne with her legs open, pussy on offer, breasts full. Little by little, the imagined sensations of soft skin, moist hair and oozing fluids began to take hold of him. The picture inside his head was like a Hieronymus Bosch painting in which every figure had his sister's face. His swollen cock was brushing against his flabby belly. He wanked furiously in a bid to escape the horror. It was not the first time he had done it while thinking about Jeanne, but it had never been brutal, bestial like this. He ejaculated, and it was like putting a knife through her heart.

It was true Jeanne and Olivier had slept together, but contrary to what Rodolphe had imagined, they had not made love. After he went off in a huff carrying the bottle under his arm, the two of them had sat in silence for a while without touching, cut off from the world in a place that belonged to them alone. Things had moved on since their first encounter the previous day; there was no sense of surprise any more, no reference to the past, no doubts. What they had just done belonged to the realm of ritual, of solemn ceremony, and they were left feeling purified. Olivier poured himself a large glass of wine. He wanted more, even more. A surge of heat ran from his heart to his head and back again. Why had he ever given up drinking? Why had he given up believing?

'It's been a long time, you know.'

'Yes, I know.'

'Did you think we would ever see one another again?'

'Sometimes, but I tried not to think about it. Things never happen if you're waiting for them.'

Olivier drank another glass. It was his heart he was filling up; it had run dry so long ago. With every gulp, he felt himself blossoming like a flower after a day in the sun.

'So what happens now?'

'No idea. We go to bed, sleep, carry on.'

He let himself be guided to Jeanne's room, bringing the bottle and glass with him. He knew he would not sleep until the bottle was empty.

The bed was unmade, the sheets and covers bundled on the floor. He placed the bottle and glass on the floor and lay down with his arms behind his neck, his head resting on the single pillow. He could hear water running in the bathroom where Jeanne had gone. The light from the half-open door was like a lemon-yellow streak across the darkness of the room. To the left of it loomed the dark mass of a chest of drawers piled high with clothes and to the right of the bed, a desk could be seen laden with files, books and other miscellany. Compared with the rest of the flat, which was fairly tidy, the mess in the bedroom was surprising. Olivier emptied the last of the bottle into his glass and downed it in one. In a few minutes, Jeanne would come and lie next to him on the bed. She would snuggle up to him like a pussycat. He would wrap his arm around her shoulders, plant a kiss on her neck, smell the scent of her hair ... In all likelihood this was going to happen, but even so he could not bring himself to believe it. He had run over this scene so many times in his head that he could not conceive of it happening in real life. He felt utterly unprepared and clumsy, just like the first time they made love, in the cabin. He had no idea what he would say to her, or how to do it without saying anything. His body was not obeying orders. He needed to move with the lightness of a dancer, but felt as heavy as an anvil. It was all he could do to wiggle his fingertips. He was sinking into the bed. The archive footage of the 'bird man' showed him jumping off the Eiffel Tower only to crash down seconds later. They said the impact of the body made a crater several centimetres deep ...

When Jeanne emerged from the bathroom, the bird man was snoring loudly with his mouth wide open and his limbs sprawled like a starfish across the bed.

'Blimey, you're getting into the Christmas spirit early, aren't you?'

Olivier could think of nothing to say in response and settled for a shrug. It was quarter to nine in the morning. He had ordered a coffee in the bistro and subsequently drank four glasses of calvados in quick succession. He needed to blow away the cobwebs that had formed in his head during the night. Now things were beginning to look up. He was waiting for the corner shop to open so he could buy a bottle of something to take back up to the flat, along with a few croissants to make him look respectable.

Jeanne had still been asleep when he woke up. The only part of her that could be seen under the covers was the dark mass of her hair, among which he spotted a single white strand. He slipped soundlessly out of bed and headed into the bathroom. He did not shower, and had not changed his clothes in two days. He looked like an escaped convict with his stubbly chin, purplish bags under his eyes and cracked lips. He dared not run the taps for fear of waking Jeanne. In any case, there was no point trying to do anything before he had had a drink. Years of practice had taught him how to tackle the depression that hits the alcoholic the moment he wakes: block everything out until you've got the first drink down you. Wearing his socks and holding his shoes in one hand, he tiptoed out of the room, put on his coat, took the keys from the door and raced out onto the street.

The bistro windows were decorated with fake snow and grotesque Father Christmases wreathed in holly as lethal as barbed wire. Stringy bits of tinsel on their umpteenth annual outing from the shoebox hung sadly along the walls. Full of festive cheer, in other words. Punters puffed like seals as they came in, tapping the crust of dirty snow from their shoes and peeling off layers of scarves and hats. Regulars greeted the owner by his first name, and ordered something hot.

Olivier glanced at his watch: 9.10 a.m. He left a few coins on the table and walked out. He headed to the corner shop first. As the door opened, it set an old-fashioned bell tinkling and a little old woman emerged from the back room. Olivier asked for a bottle of vodka. The snow and white sky, evoking the atmosphere of a Russian novel, put the idea in his head, even though he was not especially keen on the spirit. The corner shop must not have sold very much of it because it took her an age to dig out a bottle. At the bakery, the customary hysteria was already in full swing. The owner was telling off each member of her staff in turn as they went to and fro carrying Yule logs bursting with cream and dotted with figurines of dwarves and toadstools.

'Honestly, what a bunch of good-for-nothings! Today of all days! I hope you don't have to put up with nonsense like this, Monsieur.'

Olivier was tempted to reply, 'As it happens, I'm an alcoholic and a murderer, so no, my problems are not of that nature.' He ordered six all-butter croissants.

He felt cheerful, happy and free, like a tourist visiting a parallel world. He didn't wait until he was inside the flat to open the bottle. He took a good swig at the foot of the stairs by the letter boxes, at the risk of being caught by a neighbour. That made it even more thrilling. He tore up the stairs like a kid playing knock down ginger.

Rodolphe was sitting motionless at the table with a face like a runny omelette. Jeanne could be heard moving pots and pans around in the kitchen.

'Morning, warm croissants!'

'Morning, Olivier. You're a well brought-up boy. I'm not.'

Rodolphe grabbed the paper bag, took out a croissant and stuffed half of it into his mouth. Olivier went into the kitchen to find Jeanne. She was smiling, brushing her hair back. Tiny wrinkles spread from the corners of her eyes. Olivier lightly kissed her lips.

'You OK?'

'I'm great. I'm going to have a shower and get changed. I look like a complete tramp.'

'Why don't you bring your bag over here? It would make life simpler.'

He felt a vague sense of unease coming over him as he entered his mother's flat and he had to resort to the bottle of vodka still in his pocket to overcome it. Alcohol was a miracle cure, cleansing the wounds of body and soul. The key was to make sure you never ran out.

Roland's ghost had left the bathroom and it was now just another bathroom, albeit a rather dingy one. He lathered himself up from head to toe, carefully shaved and put on clean clothes. He shoved all his belongings into his bag and shut the door behind him, determined never to set foot in the place again.

Of the six croissants, Rodolphe had scoffed five, but he had said sorry. He was now getting ready to go out. 'I've got shopping to do', he had announced mysteriously. He and Jeanne had argued for half an hour over the evening's menu. She would have preferred to keep it simple, but he was adamant.

'Crime or no crime, it's Christmas!'

Olivier arrived towards the end of the discussion and volunteered to take care of drinks. Jeanne was happy to cook but categorically refused to queue up at the shops with every other Tom, Dick and Harry.

'Fine, I'll go then! It's easy. I go in tapping my stick against the floor and yell, "Can anybody help me?" Does the trick every time. It's not a stick, it's a magic wand.'

With Rodolphe gone and Jeanne getting ready, Olivier was suddenly besieged by annoying little questions: What should he do about Odile? The lawyer? Emmaus? The undertakers? His good mood was retreating in the face of this barrage of question marks. It took three good glasses of vodka to push them back, and even then he could not oust them completely. Every who, what, where, when and how was momentarily shelved in a corner of his mind, but they could come back at any time. He had to stay on his toes. It would all have to be sorted out at some point, but not now. He had already drunk three-quarters of the bottle and it was only twenty to eleven. He put it away in his bag and zipped it shut.

In order to avoid the crowds already thronging through the centre of town, Jeanne and Olivier had made their way to the park by the Saint-Cyr road, skirting the Orangery and the gates opposite the Swiss Pond. Apart from a few dedicated joggers in racing stripes who breathlessly overtook them, there was no one else out walking. At this time, normal people were massing outside shop windows by the dozen. The fresh snow squeaked beneath their feet like potato starch. The sky and earth vied with each other in their whiteness. As they reached the Grand Canal, whose huge cross-shape was chrome-plated with ice, Olivier recognised the Versailles he had always known: immovable, its proud geometry squaring up to the sky, defying time. It was beautiful, but as stiff as a corpse. They decided to walk around the lake, keeping the chateau behind them. Beneath trees sketched in big, wild strokes of charcoal, they heard creatures moving, a bird flying off a branch in a puff of white powder.

'You're not cold, are you?'

'No, I'm fine.'

They said nothing more until they reached the end of the canal, turning to look at the chateau whose black windows returned their stare. They were like Rodolphe's eyes.

'I wonder why the revolutionaries didn't raze it all to the ground.'

'Kill the father, keep the inheritance.'

'Still, it's like a big fat raspberry at the world. The only interesting thing about this town is that it makes you want to get the hell out as fast as you can.'

'And then you come back.'

Olivier picked up a branch and lobbed it onto the frozen surface of the water. The wood slid across the ice before wobbling to a stop like the needle of a compass.

'What is it about boys that makes them have to hurl things? Stones, bits of wood ...'

'It's a way of propelling yourself into the future, working out how far you can go. Shall we carry on?'

Olivier must have come this way hundreds of times, most often by bike and in summer, when the banks of the canal were transformed into an impressionist painting with loved-up couples and families dotted about on the green grass, watching the boats leaving trails in the water like scissors cutting through a length of silk. The boys would pretend to try to capsize the skiffs while the girls clung on with both hands, shrieking. People ate ice creams ...

'Do you think the café by the jetty will be open?'

'I doubt it. We'll find out when we go past.'

Olivier quickened his pace. He was regretting not having brought the bottle of vodka with him. Little by little as the alcohol wore off, the past was rising to the surface, bringing with it a host of black thoughts. As expected, the café was shut and they almost ran out of the park onto Boulevard de la Reine. They entered the first bar they came to. The noise, people and heat hit them like opening an oven door. Olivier ordered a double whisky and Jeanne a tea.

'Are you OK?'

'I'm fine, I'm fine! I was just thinking about all the stupid things I have to sort out. Emmaus, the lawyer, the funeral ...'

'Don't think about it. You can't do anything for the next two days anyway. You should call your wife.'

'What for?'

'I don't know, to set her mind at ease, to set your own mind at ease.'

'Yes, you're right. Only I'm sick of telling myself I "must do this" or "should do that". I want to just be here, in the now.'

'But you are! I'm here, stop worrying. Ring your wife. We can sort out the rest later.'

Jeanne took his hand, her fingers becoming entwined with his. He could feel her energy flowing into him, as warm and comforting as the alcohol pumping through his veins once more.

'Sorry, bit of a blip. Want anything else? I think I'll have another drink.'

After leaving the flat, Rodolphe had gone straight to Arlette's place near Gare des Chantiers. She was a respectable prostitute with her own property, where she worked for herself servicing a trouble-free, regular clientele of bachelors and retired men. He had brought her a box of her favourite liqueur chocolates.

'Thanks, Rodolphe, that's kind of you, but I don't have a lot of time to give you seeing as I'm not dressed yet and I've got a load of shopping to do for our Christmas Eve meal; I've got to buy presents for my niece and nephew, plus I'm in charge of bringing the snails. And with the shops as busy as they are!'

'That's not what I've come for. I wanted to wish you a merry Christmas and chat for a little while.'

'If you like, we can talk while I'm getting ready. Just come into the bathroom.'

Arlette's one-bedroom flat was furnished with the smell of detergent, bleach, polish, soap and perfumes as heady as they were cheap. Its cleanliness was the best possible advert for her services. Everything you touched was soft, silky, squashy, like her body. You got your money's worth with Arlette: clean inside and out.

'Go on then, what do you have to tell me?'

Rodolphe could hear the water rippling in the tub and the wet slap of the bath mitt. She must be washing her bottom. There was no need to be embarrassed in front of him.

'What would you say if I told you I'd killed a man?'

'Have you done something stupid?'

'No, just supposing.'

'Well, I'd tell you it was none of my business. These things are best kept to yourself. Anyway, you wouldn't be the first. You know, before I moved here, I got around a bit! I've had a few tough nuts in my time! But the things they tell me after a few drinks go in one ear and out the other. I get it out, recycle it, otherwise I'd have become a public dumping ground in no time. Why are you asking anyway?'

'No reason, just to see what happens when you say that to someone.'

'OK … Well, you'll have to ask someone else for your statistics, because I'm not your average woman in the street. Can't you think of something more cheerful to talk about?'

'Sorry. So tell me, what are you going to buy your niece and nephew?'

'He wants a video game, I don't know what, it's got a Japanese name, and she wants a metronome because she's learning to play the piano. Weird presents for little kids, don't you think?'

A streaming sound followed by a sucking noise let him know she was getting out of the bath. The talk after that was limited to banal chit-chat about the weather, all this money everyone was spending on Christmas when there were so many starving poor people but, even so, there was nothing wrong with having a bit of fun once in a while, and so on and so forth.

They went their separate ways at the corner of the road. Arlette planted a smacker on his lips before climbing onto the bus. People tittered as they passed the fat blind man with the serious face and a streak of bright-red lipstick across his mouth.

On their way back upstairs with their arms full of bottles (several days' worth of champagne, wine and spirits), Jeanne and Olivier bumped into Madeleine. She was standing on the second-floor landing with one hand on the banister, blocking their way.

'Ah! I've just been to your flat, as it happens. I said to myself, "Poor Monsieur Olivier, all alone for Christmas. Even if he's not in the party spirit, it'll still be nice to ask him round for a drink." Hello, Mademoiselle Mangin.'

'That's kind of you, Madeleine, but …'

'Oh, it's fine, I understand! I can see you're in good hands. The young with the young, the old with the old, that's what I always say. All that matters is that you're not on your own – it happens soon enough, after all!'

The old woman made no move to get out of their way. She seemed to be enjoying watching them bending under the weight of their boxes of bottles.

'That's what's great about being young: you make friends quickly. Is your brother well, Mademoiselle Mangin?'

'Very well, very well. Please excuse us, Madame Lasson, but these are quite heavy …'

'Of course! Come through, come through! What an old blabbermouth I am!'

She left them just enough room to squeeze between her and the banisters. Her voice followed them like a yapping dog as they continued up the stairs.

'You enjoy yourselves, and have a happy Christmas!'

'Happy Christmas to you too, Madeleine!'

As soon as they got in, Olivier poured himself a large glass of warm vodka. Jeanne started putting the champagne into the fridge.

'The old bitch spends all her time on the stairs. It's like she lives there.'

'Oh well. One day she'll miss a step and it'll be bye-bye Madeleine!'

'I doubt it. Creatures like her are indestructible.'

Olivier sipped his drink while lapping up the sight of the bottles lined up on the kitchen table. There were enough to keep his spirits up for some time to come.

'Jeanne, did you notice how the crowd parted in the street to let us through?'

'Not especially.'

'But they did! Like the sea in *The Ten Commandments*.'

'Maybe. We were walking quickly.'

'That's not the reason. It was as if they could tell we weren't from here. There was a kind of respect. Think of the guy in Nicolas. You saw how much effort he put into helping us choose the wines.'

'Given the amount of money you were putting his way, it's hardly surprising.'

'No, no, they can tell. They can tell there's something special about us.'

'You sound like Rodolphe when you talk like that.'

'Rodolphe isn't wrong all the time. He certainly picks up a lot more than he lets on.'

'That's for sure. A bit too much, even. Well, well, speak of the devil ...'

They could hear Rodolphe's voice at the front door. It sounded as if he was in one of his moods.

'No, not in the corridor! Put it all down on the table there.'

A delivery boy was piling up an array of jars and packets

bearing the logo of a smart deli. Rodolphe was red in the face. He took short shallow breaths as he unbuttoned his coat.

'Ah, there you are! Jeanne, can you give this boy a tip? I've got no change left.'

Jeanne did as she was asked and the delivery boy vanished. Rodolphe fell back into an armchair, mopping his brow.

'Fucking idiots …. what a bunch of fucking idiots!'

'What is it? What's up? Show me … What's that on your mouth?'

'What do you mean?'

'Lipstick. Geranium-red lipstick.'

'Lipstick … Ah, so that's why! People have been sniggering around me all day. Arseholes, not one of them pointed it out to me …'

Rodolphe wiped his mouth with the back of his sleeve and continued grumbling.

'Did you meet someone?'

'Yeah, a friend. I'm allowed, aren't I? Anyway, let's get down to business. I bought all ready-made stuff; there's only the snails to go in the oven. Let's not wait till midnight to start the blowout! I'm hungry, and even more thirsty! Olivier, are we all sorted on that front?'

'All set – we've got enough to last us through a siege.'

'Let's not waste any time then, we'll get cracking. Jeanne, why don't you put some music on, something jolly, like Fauré's *Requiem*. I want to hear the voice of the angels. I like angels, me.'

Rodolphe had insisted on getting out candles, a tablecloth, the good china, crystal glasses and silverware. He wanted a proper Christmas, especially since there were three of them this time instead of two, as in previous years. That had not stopped him stuffing himself like a pig and drinking like a fish. Like his shirt, the table in front of him was spotted with stains of various origins. Snail and langoustine shells and quail carcasses were piled up in fragile pyramids either side of his plate. He was making such a frantic effort to gorge himself, it was impossible not to look upon it as a kind of suicide. When his mouth was not full of food, it let out noises like rumbling pipework or told consistently awful puns. On the rare occasions he addressed Jeanne or Olivier, he never gave them a chance to respond. As soon as one CD stopped, he shouted for another. There was something almost moving about this desire to fill everything, his mouth, his stomach, his ears. He was like a bricklayer building a wall around himself, on the lookout for the tiniest cracks. By the end of the meal, he had cut himself off completely, and pretended to be pleased about the fact. Jeanne had only picked at her dinner and filled two ashtrays. Meanwhile Olivier nursed his drink and waited for it all to be over.

'Ah, kids! Praise be to the little baby Jesus! This is nice, isn't it? The three of us, all the family together. Because we are family, aren't we? A real one, with skeletons in the cupboard and everything!'

'Rodolphe, you've been a pain in the arse all through dinner. Can you give it a rest?'

'What? We've got no secrets any more. I just say what I think. But what about you two – do you think what you say?'

'And what is it we say?'

'It's all, "Good morning, good evening, please, thank you, you're welcome". But you don't believe a word you're saying! You don't give a damn about anyone but yourselves. You're unbearable to be around; you have no idea how excluded and ignored you make other people feel! You've only got one heart between the two of you. You're a freak of nature, like those sheep with five legs or calves with two heads.'

'You're talking absolute rubbish. It's you who does everything to cut yourself off by making yourself out to be worse than you really are. You've never come to terms with your blindness. You're angry at the whole world.'

'That's not true! I've got a big heart, a heart in proportion to my body, a huge heart!'

Banging his fist against the table, Rodolphe sent his plate flying off to smash on the floor. His baggy jowls were quivering and he was white with rage.

'Do you think it's fun playing blind man's bluff all by yourself? Huh?'

Olivier was enthralled, following the scene as if watching a film. The candle flames made stars dance around the rim of the glasses, on the blades of the knives, in Jeanne's eyes and Rodolphe's glasses. The performance was pitch perfect, the feelings expressed so realistically he almost broke into applause. It called to mind a Greek tragedy, leagues apart from the phone conversation he had had with Odile just before dinner, which was unfunny slapstick. Even the tone of his wife's voice had sounded ridiculous to him. She was going spare with worry, what was he doing? Where was he? Why wasn't he returning her calls? Why didn't he ring her?

He had felt like hanging up straight away. Out of the goodness

90

of his heart he went to the trouble of thinking up a lie, telling her he had run into an old school pal who had been keeping him company.

She could understand that, surely. No, of course he hadn't done anything stupid, of course he still loved her and yes, he promised to call her more often. Putting the phone down, he wished he had never called. In Odile's world, he felt dirty.

Jeanne was picking up the pieces of broken plate. Rodolphe had calmed down. Now only his lower lip was trembling, as if he was about to cry.

'Sorry, Jeanne; my apologies, Olivier. I don't know what came over me. All those people today who couldn't care less. Let's start again, shall we? ... It's time for some presents! Come on then, Olivier, pop the cork!'

Rodolphe hauled himself up, supporting himself on the back of his chair, and zigzagged his way to his bedroom, emerging a few minutes later laden with packages tied with ribbon. Olivier filled the champagne flutes. Jeanne disappeared and returned with a large box of her own.

'Right, let's put this lot on the table. I'll film you opening your presents. This one's for my beloved big sister and the other's for you, Olivier.'

'That's very kind of you, Rodolphe. I'm so sorry, I completely forgot, I haven't ...'

'Oh, it doesn't matter! Just having you here is enough for us. Open it, open it!'

Rodolphe turned the camcorder on, pointing the lens at the rustling paper. The box Olivier was opening carried the logo of an arms maker and contained a hunting horn.

'So ...?'

'It's a lovely horn, but I have to say I'm not quite sure I get it ...'

'Of course you do! It's Roland's *cor*, you know, the horn he blew at the Battle of Roncevaux Pass. Or is it Roland's corpse? You have to admit it's a good one, isn't it?'

Rodolphe burst out laughing. His fat belly wobbled, giving the camera a rocking motion. The shot itself would not be a good one.

'What about yours, Jeanne? Do you like it?'

In her palm she held a glass ball, which she set down on a mahogany pedestal table.

'Is it a crystal ball?'

'You guessed it! I bought it in a new-age shop. So, what can you see in it?'

'Nothing.'

'What do you mean, nothing? It came with a guarantee. If you can't see your future, I'll take it back.'

'There's no need. It'll make a very nice paperweight.'

'Give it here. I bet I can see better with my hands than you can with your eyes.'

Rodolphe put down the camcorder and took hold of the ball.

'It needs warming up a bit ... there, I'm beginning to make something out ... it's still a bit blurry but it's getting clearer ... There it is! It's blue, lots of blue ... the sky or the police? ... The sea, perhaps ... Nothing, emptiness, nothing but emptiness, a long, long drop ...'

'That'll do, Rodolphe. Very funny. Why don't you open your present?'

'Oh, yes. There you go, have your ball back; it works fine. So ... Oh, it's big!'

His podgy fingers tore at the paper and the sellotape holding the lid shut.

'What is it?'

'A set of bathroom scales.'

'Bathroom scales? For weighing? Fantastic! I'll try them out straight away.'

He put the scales down in the middle of the floor, clambered onto them and struck a pose like a statue.

'How much do I weigh?'

'A hundred and fifteen kilos.'

'Is that all? What does it go up to?'

'One fifty.'

'I should manage that within a month or two. Thank you, Jeanne, thanks very much. I'll start work right away. Bring out the Yule log and let the champagne flow!'

Olivier had reached the stage when he could just as easily stop as carry on drinking. The only reason he kept draining his glass was to prolong this state of grace. He did not stutter or stammer, there was just a certain slowness to his actions. Something like the woozy feeling divers describe on returning from the deep. Everything had a deep-sea look to it, in fact; objects seemed to glow from within, shining among the shadows which danced on the walls, and Rodolphe's body was a humungous jellyfish which had washed up on the sofa, his chocolate-smeared mouth letting out regular snores. Olivier went to stand with Jeanne who was leaning her head against the window, smoking. As he placed his hand on her shoulder, he could feel she was shivering. It could be no later than midnight, and there were lights in most windows. Silhouettes flitted across the yellow rectangles like shadow puppets. Jeanne stubbed out her cigarette against the wet glass, unfazed by the ashes falling onto the floor.

'This is my last Christmas here.'

'Did you see that in your crystal ball?'

'No, even better, I've decided.'

'You want to go away?'

'Yes, somewhere far from here.'

They were holding on to one another and had unconsciously started to sway as if on the bridge of a ship, gently rocking from side to side.

'I want to feel warm, all over.'

'Come here.'

The last candle went out as day began to break. Wrapped in a blanket, Olivier watched the blue slowly creeping into the room. Rodolphe was no longer on the sofa; he must have finally dragged himself off to bed. The scales were still in the middle of the carpet, directly beneath the light. The last few patches of darkness clung on around the ceiling rose. The table had not been cleared; the set had not been dismantled. Olivier was reminded of Pompeii, of mineralised life. He felt as if he were himself made of stone. A statuesque silence reigned over his body. His eyelids no longer seemed able to shut. He had not slept. They had made love without reserve or restraint, like two flailing swimmers dragging each other down towards the abyss amid the foam of crashing waves. Just like the people in the print of *The Raft of the Medusa* on the wall opposite him. He never imagined Jeanne's body could unleash such a tempest. The truth was he had never given a moment's thought to Jeanne's body. She was not all mind after all; she had breasts, buttocks and a vagina, and this revelation left him as bewildered as the day he lost his virginity.

Olivier took a swig of Williamine. The pear liqueur was just what was needed, a rush of white heat. He had started drinking when he was very young, almost as soon as he arrived in Réunion; rum, mixed with fruit juice to begin with, moving on to *rhum arrangé* with added grains of rice which fermented and took it up to almost 70 per cent proof. Since the age of sixteen, he had loved nothing and nobody but alcohol. No woman – and Lord knows there had been a few – had been powerful enough to defeat it. He only stopped drinking because his gamma GT levels had gone through the roof and clots in his legs were making it hard for him to walk. An enforced vacation, putting the tired old horse out to pasture for a few years. Now it was time to get back in the saddle. It was a long journey to the island. He knew that Jeanne would never say anything about his drinking. She didn't view it as competition, or as a handicap. Olivier drank; he could just as easily not drink; it was all the same to her. The last trickle of pear liqueur felt like a teardrop, the kind that comes when you're brimming with happiness.

Over the next two days, Jeanne and Olivier left the bed only to carry out a limited number of rapid commando missions to the closest corner shop. Their timetable consisted of having sex, drinking and grazing on foods that required no preparation. Next door there lived a bear, Rodolphe, whom they could hear coming and going, growling, slamming doors, turning the TV and hi-fi up as far as they would go, who constantly howled his presence and yet didn't dare knock on their door. They were unfazed; the sound of the waves they imagined lapping around them easily drowned out Rodolphe's ranting and raving.

'Lying in the shade of the filao trees fringing the white sand beaches of Mauritius is like sleeping under a fan of light feathers. There's nowhere else like it. The sand foams at your feet and the silence rings in your ears.'

'And the fish, tell me more about the fish!'

This continued until the 27th, the day of the funeral. It had turned milder and the snow was melting, leaving patches here and there like bubbles on dishwater. A note slipped under the door marked for Olivier's attention had coldly informed him of the time and place. Madeleine's handwriting was just like the woman herself: jagged, pointy, sharp-edged. Olivier did not think it appropriate to bring Jeanne, still less Rodolphe, who had nonetheless done his best to twist Olivier's arm.

'Go on! It'll get me out of the house, and besides I love cemeteries.'

In the end he had gone alone to the church, where he found Madeleine waiting. Since they were the only ones accompanying the deceased to her final resting place, Madeleine could not give free rein to her hatred of Olivier. Circumstances dictated that they share a kind of common spirit. The religious ceremony was over in no time and they soon found themselves sitting in the back of the hearse on either side of the coffin, from which the wreath tied with purple ribbon slipped at every bend in the road. The smell was nauseating. Olivier retrieved a hip flask from his pocket and took a long swig of whisky while the old woman watched, appalled.

'On a day like this! Have you no shame?'

Olivier shrugged. What was so special about today? For the people wading through sludge on the street, today was like yesterday in every respect, and tomorrow would doubtless be no different. It was just another day. What did they care about the long black car skidding past on the slippery tarmac? It meant no more to them than the sight of the binmen picking up rubbish. Olivier shared their point of view. There were no stars in life, only walk-on actors. They arrived at the cemetery in Gonnards, a suburban neighbourhood in miniature where pitiful or pretentious houses called 'Mon Rêve' or 'Ça Me Suffit' were set out in neat rows. The tomb where Antoine Verdier already lay was yawning. Two gravediggers stood beside it smoking a cigarette and leaning on their shovels. Once the coffin had been lowered into the bottom of the hole, Madeleine did something strange. She grabbed hold of Olivier's arm and leaned so far over the edge of the grave that Olivier had to pull her back to stop her falling in. A few stones rained onto the oak lid of the coffin.

'Can't wait your turn, Madeleine?'

'I ... I just wanted to see.'

'See what?'

'I don't know.'

She was not crying, but her eyes had misted over. They soon

regained their evil glint and she let go of Olivier's arm as if she had just touched a hot iron. The man from the undertaker's offered to take them back into town. Madeleine agreed. Olivier opted to make his own way back. They parted without saying goodbye. He drained his flask while watching the cemetery workers shovelling. Not a single flower on the surrounding tombs had survived the frost.

There was not much difference between the place he had just left and the city streets he was now treading. The only exception was that here, the dead were living. Olivier had the impression of flicking through a family album, a series of black and white photos that brought back no memories. Rue des Chantiers seemed to go on forever, as if he was walking against a treadmill. He stopped three times for refreshments in bars along the way. Between pit stops, he repeated to himself: 'Scoot, take off, get the hell out.'

It was Jeanne who opened the door to him. Evidently all was not well. From inside the flat, he could hear Rodolphe yelling.

'Who is it? ... Who is it?'

'Olivier.'

'Ah, about time too! Just the person I want to see!'

Olivier took off his coat in the hallway.

'What's up with him?'

'The police came.'

'What?'

'They found Roland's body, a guy out walking his dog in the woods. They put out a photo and a shopkeeper recognised him. He told them Roland had bought a pair of shoes and that he was with a blind man. He remembered the two of them very clearly because they were both legless. He gave a perfect description of Rodolphe.'

'Shit ...'

Rodolphe appeared in the doorway. He was like a lump of jelly in the hands of a Parkinson's sufferer.

'You can say that again! Shit, shit, shit! The game's up for me now, isn't it?'

'Stop shouting! Let's not stand here.'

Jeanne moved them into the living room. Olivier opened the bottle he had just bought and offered a glass to Rodolphe, who shrugged it away. Olivier knocked back his drink. He felt strangely calm and collected.

'Were you here, Jeanne?'

'No, I was out doing the shopping.'

'What did you say to them, Rodolphe?'

'What do you think I said? We were seen together in ten different places that day, I could hardly deny it!'

'Did you tell them he came here?'

'Of course I did! Someone might have seen us; how the hell should I know? I said he came home with me, I gave him some money and he left straight away. That's it. But they've called me in for questioning tomorrow and you can bet they'll put the heat on me. They're not stupid, they know what they're about. But if it goes too far, there's no way I'm carrying the can for this!'

'There's no need to get worked up, Rodolphe, I understand completely. If, like you say, it goes too far, I'll do the right thing.'

'Oh you will, will you? And why should I believe you? I'm not just going to sit there and let you frame me! You're not landing this on me – I won't stand for it!'

'You've got me all wrong, Rodolphe. I've got nothing against you.'

'Well, I've got plenty against you! And you, Jeanne, what have you got to say for yourself? Huh?'

'I'm thinking, all right?'

'Oh, she's thinking! Here, give me something to drink, that'll help me "think" too.'

'You'd be better off keeping a clear head. You've got yourself in enough of a state as it is. This is all ridiculous anyway. If you stick to what you've already said, nothing's going to happen.'

'Yeah, right! I'm the last person who saw him alive. You think they're going to let me go, just like that?'

'And how exactly would you, a poor blind man, have dragged him into the forest several kilometres from here, in the middle of the night, strangled him and then walked home again? No one's going to believe that.'

Rodolphe said nothing. He rubbed the end of his nose and frowned. Catching Jeanne's eye, Olivier gathered it would be best to leave the two of them alone. She was used to dealing with her brother, and having Olivier there would only wind Rodolphe up. It was for the best anyway, he was tired and wanted only one thing: to lie down on Jeanne's bed.

With his head on the pillow and his hands folded over his stomach, he could hear their voices through the dividing wall without making out the individual words. From time to time Rodolphe's rose up a notch, but Jeanne's steady, constant, almost hypnotic murmur calmed him down again. She was like a horse-breaker patiently taming a skittish beast. The fact was Olivier felt completely detached from what was happening. He was surprised at himself, but it was true. What Rodolphe might or might not do made no difference to him. He had been in the same frame of mind since first thing that morning. It was the same at the church, the same at the cemetery and the same in town. Exhaustion. He was all too familiar with the particular brand of weariness that follows the euphoria of drunkenness, a weariness that leaves you stranded on the line, anaesthetised to the point you can no longer tell friend from enemy, hot from cold, being from nothingness. What on earth did he have to be afraid of? We're all innocent when we're asleep.

*

*He had a long white beard that tickled his navel. Madeleine was furiously digging a large hole in the sand which the waves kept filling in again. She was naked, she had eyes like a fly and she kept bailing out the water between each flood of foam, cursing to herself. He kept telling her, 'It's deep enough, Madeleine!' but she wouldn't listen, she kept digging, digging ...*

'Olivier?'

Jeanne's face appeared as a white patch in the middle of his dream, which whorled away like the curls of smoke from the cigarette she held to her lips.

'What time is it?'

'I'm not sure, three or four o'clock. Rodolphe's calmed down. Are you OK?'

'I'm not sure. Probably, yes.'

'I've managed to convince him to stand by his story. He's agreed on one condition: you have to leave.'

'Oh.'

'I don't want you to.'

'Let's go together.'

'We can't. I know what he's like. He'll blab everything to the police.'

'What then?'

Jeanne took a long puff on her cigarette. As the end glowed red, it lit her fingertips, her mouth and the end of her nose. The ashes fell onto her skirt. She swept them off with the back of her hand. Set in a surround of silence, every little detail seemed deeply significant.

'I don't think it was you who killed Roland.'

'Well, who was it, then? ... Rodolphe?'

'He's sick enough to have stitched you up. He hates you.'

The thought had not even crossed Olivier's mind. He had been so convinced of his own guilt when he lost his memory that there had been no room for doubt. For the last five days, he had put himself in a murderer's skin, and now he had to reconsider everything. It was absurd, but the idea he might be innocent irked him.

'How can we be sure?'

'You had no reason to strangle Roland, but he did.'

'When you're having an alcoholic episode, you're capable of anything, you know.'

'So is Rodolphe, and that's when he's stone-cold sober.'

'But why not just shop me to the police that morning? Why help us dispose of the body? It doesn't add up.'

'For fun, for his own twisted pleasure, and also because he's scared of me now. He knows I'm capable of anything too. He's spun a web and got himself trapped in it. He's trying to find an amicable solution. You leave and he keeps his mouth shut.'

'Fine, so why don't I go and you follow on afterwards?'

'He'll never leave us alone. He and I have always been at loggerheads. Sooner or later it was bound to come to this. For years he's had a hold over me, smothering me. I don't think I can put up with him another twenty-four hours. I didn't care before – I just let him drag me down a little further every day. And then you came back. I want to live, Olivier, I want to live with you. Chances like this don't come around twice.'

'So?'

'Rodolphe is the only suspect.'

'And?'

'He has a long history of depression. Right up until last year he was seeing a psychiatrist who could confirm he has a tendency towards paranoia ... and suicidal thoughts.'

'Ah, I see ...'

Olivier was coming back to earth, this earth where people live a little and die a lot. Exit Rodolphe! Jeanne's gaze was clear; no one could have guessed what she was plotting beneath that pale brow. It was almost something to admire. He stood up, went straight to the chest of drawers and pulled out a bottle of he no longer knew what. He had gone back to his little habits, stashing bottles all over the place so he could always be sure of having one to hand.

'Right. And how are you planning to go about ... committing your brother's suicide?'

'I don't know, something simple, obvious. The window, maybe.'

'The window?'

'Yes. We'll leave it wide open, he'll try to shut it, and one of us will come up behind him and push him.'

'Who'll push him?'

'It would be better if you did it.'

'Uh ... I'm not sure what to say to that. Why me?'

'Because I won't be there.'

'It gets better and better! Listen, Jeanne, I love you, I adore you, but you have to admit—'

'I'm not trying to wriggle out of it, Olivier. Listen to me. He has to be home alone for his suicide to be believable. Right now, you pack up your things and tell Rodolphe you're going – he's won. You go back to your mother's. Half an hour later, I'll go out to pick something up from the shops. On my way past, I'll drop you the keys. You come back over here. He'll be in the living room with *Countdown* on; you know how he turns the volume right up. You open the window of the dining room and wait for him to come over. You push him out, turn off the TV, go home, locking the door behind you, and you sit tight. Simple as that.'

'Simple as that ... it's pure madness!'

'Olivier! He's got you in the palm of his hand. It's you who could end up going to prison instead of him. We have no choice!'

'But why does it have to be right now, tonight?'

'Because he's scared, because he's due to be questioned tomorrow, because he's guilty!'

'I'll never be able to do it.'

'Of course you will! You have to believe that you can because otherwise it's all over for you and me, because of him! Think how unfair that would be. We deserve another chance. This is the final test.'

'Jeanne, Jeanne … Why is there death everywhere we go?'

'So that we can live, Olivier. That's just the way it is.'


Olivier could still feel Rodolphe's clammy, limp handshake on his skin.

'It's probably better this way. Goodbye.'

The blind man said nothing. His nostrils twitched. He waited for Olivier to slam the door behind him before his breathing returned to normal.

Olivier felt he was going back to square one, back to this flat he thought he would never set foot in again. It required an enormous effort to force himself not to think about anything, to live each minute without worrying about the last or the next. His gaze settled on the bottle of Ballantine's but he refrained from unscrewing the cap. It contained all the courage he was lacking, but the situation demanded total lucidity. Unless … unless he picked up his bag and coat and took the first train or plane out of here. He seized the bottle and knocked the whisky back so quickly he almost choked. It was like a bomb going off in his stomach, a mushroom cloud rising to his brain and nuking all possibility of intelligent thought. It was exactly what he was hoping for. There were three short knocks at the door. He opened it with tears in his eyes. Jeanne looked like a faded watercolour.

'Are you all right? … Here's the key. Wait ten minutes for his programme to start … I love you.'

Olivier had just enough time to close the door and run to the sink. He threw up a yellowish liquid that burned his gullet but did him good, as did the water on his face. Now he felt empty, calm, cold. He changed his leather-soled shoes for a less noisy pair with rubber soles. He was ready to go. Just as he was about to close the door behind him, he realised he had forgotten his keys and ran back inside, cursing himself. There was no one on the stairs. The key turning in the lock made a slight click-clack but it merged with the sound of the TV, which was audible from the landing. Standing motionless in the dark hallway, Olivier got his breath back and ran his tongue over his cracked lips. He felt as if he was being held on a leash with a collar digging in around his neck. He approached the shaft of light on the threshold of the living room, and gently pushed the door. All he could see of Rodolphe was the top of his head and his fingers tapping on the arm of the chair. Olivier hugged the wall, inching towards the dining room.

'Six letters? ... Six letters as well. Over to you, Monsieur Menoux.'
'Zombie.'
'Monsieur Bismuth?'
'Zombie as well.'
'Great. Zombie: according to West Indian folklore, a corpse said to have been raised from the dead and manipulated by witchcraft. An apathetic or slow-witted person.'

Olivier was about to cross over into the dining room when Rodolphe suddenly stood up. He paused for a moment as if unsure where to go, all the while facing a petrified Olivier head-on. Eventually he went to pour himself a drink from the trolley beside the TV before returning to his armchair. The whole thing lasted only a minute or two, long enough for Olivier to see his whole life flash before his eyes.

'One hundred and eighteen plus sixty-three times seven ...'
All human thoughts had deserted Olivier's brain. He

proceeded mechanically towards the window, sliding one foot in front of the other like the Horse Guards. His hands reached the catch and flung back both panes. A gust of icy air rushed in, so cold it was as if it had teeth. Olivier took three steps back and stood at attention.

'What's ... Is someone there? ... Who's that?'

Rodolphe was on his feet again, the draught lifting one flap of his dressing gown.

'Who's there?'

*'Consonant ... vowel ... consonant ...'*

'Damn it!'

Rodolphe came closer and closer ... there was a shadow of doubt on his contorted face. His ears, nose, the pores of his skin were all on high alert. Olivier held his breath, as tightly wound as a spring. The blind man's nostrils twitched as he passed fifty centimetres in front of him. It must be the whisky he could smell, but seeing as he had just had a glass himself ... He opened his arms to the darkness like a bloated Christ and tried to pull the window closed, his belly touching the cast-iron guard rail. Olivier jumped forward, arms outstretched, eyes shut. He heard a kind of mooing followed almost immediately by a dull thud, and pressed his back against the wall.

*'Well done, Monsieur Bismuth! Spot on!'*

The black butterflies fluttering beneath his eyelids turned bright yellow when he opened his eyes. He would never be able to shut them again. He crossed the room, turned off the TV, rushed out of the flat, turned the key twice in the door, crossed the landing and double-locked himself in. His ears were completely blocked up. The only sounds he heard came from within, glugs, fizzes, blubs ... He sat down on a chair facing the wall and turned on the radio, eyes wide, body tingling with boiling blood.

'I did it ... Jesus, I did it!'

He had done it. Jeanne arrived at the same time as the police, who parked their van beside a group of four or five people gathered at the foot of the building. Madeleine, who was of course one of them, saw Jeanne coming a long way off and lunged towards her.

'Oh, Mademoiselle Mangin, it's awful! Your poor brother!'

'What about him?'

'He's ... I saw the whole thing! I was looking out of my window and all of a sudden I saw something falling, just like that, bam! Right before my eyes! It was me who called the emergency services, not five minutes ago. My God!'

Jeanne pushed two or three onlookers out of the way. Two officers were kneeling beside Rodolphe. His eyes were staring up at the empty sky and a bubble of blood was forming at the corner of his mouth. His right leg was jerking.

'Please, Madame ...'

'I'm his sister. Is he ...'

'No, but it's not looking good. Francis, call an ambulance.'

'What happened?'

Madeleine elbowed her way to the front to chime in again.

'I saw the whole thing! He fell like a stone, right before my eyes! Not five minutes ago!'

'Is anyone else at home?'

'No. He was alone when I went out about twenty minutes ago.'

'Francis, Gérard, stay here and wait for the ambulance. I'll go upstairs with the lady.'

Jeanne climbed the stairs followed first by the police officer and second by Madeleine, who would not stop saying 'My God'.

Jeanne breathed a little more easily when the key turned twice in the lock.

'Do you lock it when you go out?'

'No – he does. My brother's a very anxious person.'

The three of them entered the flat. The dining-room window

was wide open and the wind was billowing the curtains. Jeanne went to shut it, but the police officer stopped her. For the time being, they were not to touch anything.

'Who does this white stick belong to?'

'My brother. Rodolphe's blind.'

'Ah … so it was an accident?'

'I doubt it. Rodolphe has been blind since birth. He's very independent.'

Shame – the cop would clearly rather have gone with his own neat hypothesis. He took a cursory look around the room before the ambulance siren was heard blaring.

'Here they are. I imagine you'd like to go with your brother?'

'Yes, of course. Can I close the window? It'll be freezing later.'

'Yeah, go ahead.'

Out on the landing, the officer briefly took down Madeleine's statement and had to tell her three times he had no further need of her. Jeanne did not need anything either; nobody required her services. Disappointed, Madeleine watched them go downstairs but could not bring herself to do the same. It couldn't just end like this! She planted her finger firmly on Olivier's doorbell.

'Ah, you're home! So you haven't heard?'

'Heard what? What is it?'

'Your neighbours across the hall, your friends …'

'What about them?'

'The gentleman, the blind one, well, he's thrown himself out of the window!'

'What are you talking about?'

'I saw the whole thing! I saw him falling right before my eyes, plain as I see you now! Bam! Like a stone!'

'Is he … is he dead?'

'Near enough! It's not a pretty sight, blood all over the pavement.'

'He's not dead? Are you sure?'

'He was still moving, but … what a question.'

'I'm just surprised, from this height …'

'You've been drinking again, haven't you? I heard all about it from your poor maman. She thought you'd given up.'

'I had. What about Jeanne – I mean his sister?'

'Well, she's at the hospital, of course!'

'Yes, of course. Thanks, Madeleine, thank you.'

'Thanks for what?'

'I don't know.'

'You don't need anything?'

'No, nothing. Goodbye.'

The old lady stared open-mouthed at the closed door before making up her mind to go home.

'They drink, they lark about, they throw themselves out of windows … What's the world coming to?'

It was a question of minutes, maybe hours if the heart held out, but beyond that there was no hope. She could stay if she wanted, but she was better off going home; they would call her when the time came. One of the laces on the junior doctor's trainers was undone. Jeanne was about to point this out to him when two stretcher-bearers came rushing through the waiting area of the emergency ward. A pale hand stuck out from under a sheet along with two feet in odd socks, one grey and the other with red and black stripes. A woman with a blue rinse who was there with her husband, whose hand was wrapped in a big bloodied bandage, muttered, 'That's a car crash, if ever I saw one.'

'And how would you know?'

'I just do.'

'Think you're so clever, don't you?'

'Well, if you'd only listened to me instead of carrying on with that electric carving knife, we wouldn't be here, would we?'

'Oh, is that right?'

Of course there was no point staying, with her bottom squeezed into this moulded plastic chair, watching the nurses' Scholl clogs dancing in front of her, but Jeanne wanted to be certain Rodolphe was dead. He was capable of anything, even coming back to life. She would not breathe freely until her brother had breathed his last. She wasn't worried about anything else. The police would pay her a visit tomorrow, that was obvious, but so what? She would just repeat everything the officer had seen with his own eyes. If necessary, she would call in Rodolphe's psychiatrist. As for the guy they had found in the woods, she knew nothing about it. All of this seemed so clear and logical it didn't even feel like lying. Destiny could get it wrong, and it was perfectly reasonable to rewrite the script if the scene wasn't up to scratch. She hadn't doubted Olivier for a moment. In spite of his fears and failings, he had risen to the task, and she thought all the better of him for it. Though he had been battered and wounded along the way, he had lost none of the fighting spirit that made them plough through life together like a horse and cart. Nobody, nothing could stand in their way.

Rodolphe was her brother, but Rodolphe had lost. Or perhaps he had won. He had never enjoyed life; it caused him too much pain. He always knew he wasn't cut out for it. He didn't have the knack. He couldn't bear the keen ones at the Institute for the Blind who were self-sufficient, excelled at everything, accomplished all kinds of feats without the aid of white sticks or dogs! He had made minimal effort, ensuring he remained as dependent as possible. Everyone had to know what a terrible handicap it was to be blind.

Jeanne fully understood and respected Rodolphe's point of view. He had never tried to be like other people; he shouted from the rooftops that he was different. It was the best strategy to adopt. One way or another, he was always going to lose. Even if Olivier had left, his victory would have killed him, and he knew it. Something had snapped between him and his sister, like an overstretched elastic band. Things could never go back to the way they were.

A homeless man was brought in, blind drunk and covered in bruises. His clothes, skin and hair were the colour of the streets, greenish, brown-black, grey. He smelt like it too, everything from petrol to urine. He kept falling over. Was his fate really more enviable than Rodolphe's?

At 21.37, the junior doctor informed her that her brother had succumbed to his injuries.

*

Olivier realised he had nothing left to drink just before eight o'clock.

He hurtled downstairs at breakneck speed but it was when he reached the shop that he came a cropper: the metal shutter was down. There was a trickle of yellow light coming out from underneath it. The old woman must still be inside. He knocked three times, then harder three times more, until the shutter came halfway up and the shopkeeper poked her head out.

'What are you banging on the shutter like that for? What do you want?'

'It's very good of you to open up for me. There are more of us than I was expecting this evening, and I'm a bit short on whisky ...'

'The same one as this morning?'

'Er ... yes.'

'Stay there.'

He couldn't help justifying himself, telling a fib before buying every bottle. It was pointless since the shopkeeper knew perfectly well he was a drunk and couldn't have cared less. And he knew that she knew. But that didn't matter, it was all part of the game, like hiding the bottles even when he was by himself. With the whisky safely in his pocket, he felt reassured, equipped for anything. He had no desire to go back up. There was no way Jeanne would be home from the hospital yet. He headed towards Le Départ, the café at Gare Rive Gauche. As a youngster, he never came here. People said it attracted the wrong sort of crowd. Instead he would meet his friends at L'Arrivée, in Gare Rive Droite. Sons of surgeons and lawyers with aristocratic names like de Beauvaroc, de Clérice, d'Alban-Michau. They probably still met up there – them, or their children. People like that had it made from birth. For a while, he had been proud to be admitted into their circle despite the fact his father was a lowly public servant. It was Jeanne who opened his eyes with a single word:

'Those guys? Cocky dodos.'

That was exactly what they were, the last survivors of their race who were inflated with pride but would never take off. L'Arrivée or Le Départ, that was the choice you had to make in Versailles. He himself had never known anything but departures. The few times he felt he had arrived corresponded with periods of total lethargy when he had no desire to go anywhere, like with Odile.

What about Rodolphe? How could he not have arrived yet? After a fall like that, he should have turned into an omelette on the pavement. What if he didn't die? What if he was only paralysed? Paralysed and mute was OK; they could stick him in a corner somewhere, but if he talked … Olivier ducked into a doorway and opened his bottle. He needed a pick-me-up before entering the café, like people who take a little nap before going to bed.

Those drinking in the café had nothing to do at home: bachelors, widowers, drunks, all on their own, except for one couple snuggled up in a corner of a banquette at the back of the room. Olivier copied the man at the next table and ordered a Ricard. Since Rodolphe wasn't dead, he would have to kill him a second time. This didn't seem an insurmountable task. It was just a pain in the arse, like having to redo your homework. One day, when he was little, he had gone fishing for frogs. In order to slay them, you had to grab them by their back legs and whack their heads against a stone. The one which took Olivier's bait stubbornly refused to die. He had had to crush the creature between two slabs to finish it off. Only afterwards did someone point out it was a toad. The two lovebirds stood up. The girl had tears in her eyes and the boy was holding a suitcase. The other customers watched them go, some nursing a half-pint, some a

Ricard, some – the most hopeless cases – a small café crème, all expecting the words 'THE END' to appear traced on the bistro's steamed-up window.

'Are you married?'

'Yes ... no.'

The man at the neighbouring table wasn't surprised by this response. He wasn't seeking any response at all; Olivier was merely a pretext for him to begin talking to himself, as often happens in café-bars after a certain time of night.

'In twenty-five years of marriage, my wife and I never left one another's side. We did everything together – the shopping, the dishes, the housework, even nothing. We sometimes went whole days without saying a word to one another, doing nothing at all, but always together.'

'Is she dead, your wife?'

'No.'

'Why are you talking about her in the past tense?'

'One day she decided to take up crochet, starting with doilies, then tablecloths, curtains, bedcovers ... bigger and bigger things. She hasn't stopped. She's like an insect weaving a thick cocoon around herself. It's weird, you know, living with an insect. They don't think the same way as us, they see things geometrically, always building things, piling them higher with one aim: to keep making ghastly little white rosettes, on and on to infinity. It's unbelievable!'

'They say insects can resist anything, even nuclear fallout.'

'That's exactly it, she's resisting! She won't take things as they are.'

'My mother used to make doilies, head rests and things. She's dead now though.'

'Of course she is ... it's never a good sign when they start to crochet.'

*

They had said everything there was to say to one another. The man went back into his shell and Olivier stood up to leave.

Outside, the sky looked like a wall of shitters covered in graffiti and mottled with rust. Its reflection in the gutter was prettier, iridescent with oil patches like the northern lights in miniature. He stood on the edge of the pavement for a while, staring up at the liquid sky like the fool in a tarot game, one foot on the edge of the cliff, the other stepping into the void, with a bundle on a stick over his shoulder and dogs nipping at his heels. Someone had once told him you became an adult the day you started avoiding puddles. He jumped in with both feet.

It took him a long time to find his road. It had been shuffled together with dozens of other roads that all looked the same. He couldn't even ask one of the few passers-by because he had forgotten what it was called. It had a corner shop on it – that was all he knew. He eventually stumbled on it when he had given up hope and resigned himself to wandering the dark maze of streets until the end of time. There was a light on at Jeanne's.

'He died around nine thirty. Nine thirty-seven, to be precise. Aren't you going to take off your coat?'

'What? ... No, I'm fine.'

Olivier had slumped into Rodolphe's armchair without even undoing his overcoat. He could not yet distinguish between inside and out. Jeanne was nibbling a slice of ham.

'Are you sure you don't want anything to eat?'

'No. So he's really dead?'

'Yes.'

'So everything's all right ...'

'For now, anyway. The police are bound to come tomorrow. They'll have to conclude it was suicide.'

'Yes … Aren't you tired?'

'No, no more than usual.'

'I am. I mean, just my body. Part of me, the energy I used pushing Rodolphe, went out of the window with him. With little Luc, there were two of us, and it was an accident. Roland – well, beats me, but with Rodolphe I knew exactly what I was doing. It's a whole different ball game.'

'Are you feeling guilty? Do you regret it?'

'No! Not at all. That's probably what surprises me most, the fact it's so easy, that it takes so little out of you, other than this tiredness …'

'On the island, we'll have all the time in the world to relax and recharge our batteries.'

'Oh yes, the island …!'

Olivier looked down at his hands. The lines on his palms formed a muddled network of roads.

'Don't you believe in it any more?'

'Yes, I just can't see it.'

'Maybe because we're already there.'

Jeanne swept knife and fork, crumbs and yogurt pot onto her tray and stood up. Olivier followed her into the kitchen. On the way, he picked up Rodolphe's crystal ball from a shelf and rolled it in his hands.

'What are we going to do with all this freedom?'

'We'll learn.'

'It'll take time.'

'Well, freedom is time.'

The tap swirl didn't work very well. The water sprayed out in a fan shape like a cat's whiskers, splattering the entire sink. Jeanne was wearing yellow rubber gloves. Olivier perched on the corner of the table. There was no future in the ball, only his grotesque face with a huge misshapen nose.

'Where am I sleeping tonight?'

'Across the hall. I think it's best for the next few days.'

'I like watching you do things, everyday, humdrum stuff.'

Jeanne pulled off her gloves, removed her apron and came to nestle against Olivier.

'We'll have days and days and days together.'

Olivier let go of the ball, which smashed on the tiled floor. Neither of them took this as a bad sign. At worst it might mean they cut themselves treading barefoot on a shard.

The man who introduced himself as Inspector Luneau didn't really fit the part. He looked more like a teacher, a primary-school head at a push, with a chinstrap beard, a pipe, a burgundy polo-neck jumper, and a notebook and pen. Jeanne was pouring him the coffee he had initially turned down.

'So you didn't know your brother had been called in for questioning today?'

'No.'

'And you don't know why either?'

'No. He didn't say anything. He seemed a bit on edge all day, but that wasn't unusual for him. I didn't think anything of it. What was he supposed to be questioned about?'

The inspector put three sugars in his coffee and slowly stirred it with a teaspoon.

'Did he spend the evening of the 22nd with you?'

'The 22nd ... Yes, he came home around six or seven. He had had quite a bit to drink. He was saying what a gift to humanity he was ... he was pissed. I decided to take a tray of food and have dinner in my room. A bit later, I heard the door slam. I read for a while and then I went to sleep.'

'So you can't say for certain that he spent the night here?'

'No. Rodolphe was very independent. He had his own life.'

Luneau pulled out a photo from his pocket. Roland looked as if he was asleep.

'Did you ever see this man with your brother?'

'No. He's not familiar. To tell the truth, I never had a clue who his friends were. I don't think he had many. He met people in passing, in bars …'

'Did he drink a lot?'

'Quite a bit, and he took prescription drugs too, Moclamine, Equanil … He was seeing a psychiatrist up until last year. The doctor could tell you more about that than I can.'

They were interrupted by the ringing of the doorbell.

'Will you excuse me?'

'Go ahead.'

Olivier was leaning against the doorframe, dishevelled and poorly shaven with a bottle of champagne in his hand.

'All right?'

'Yes.'

'Are they here?'

'Yes.'

'Shit, I wanted to drink champagne with you.'

'Now's perhaps not the time. Come back later.'

'Can I see them?'

'Best not. Go home. I'll let you know when they've gone.'

'OK … OK. But I would have liked to see them. Will you tell me what happens?'

'Of course, now go on, go.'

The inspector was jotting things in his notebook when Jeanne returned.

'One of my neighbours.'

'I see. Would you be able to give me the address of the psychiatrist your brother was treated by?'

'Of course. But you haven't told me what all this is about, the man, the photo, Rodolphe being called in …'

'This guy was found strangled in Fausses-Reposes forest and several witnesses claim to have seen your brother with him during the day on the 22nd. That's all we know.'

119

'And you think Rodolphe …'

'Oh, I don't think anything at all! I'm just gathering the facts. That's everything then. I'll leave you in peace. Thanks for the coffee.'

The champagne bubbles were fizzing under Olivier's nose, right up to the brim of his glass.

'Is that it? That's how you left it, a coffee and the bill please?'

'Yes.'

'Easy as that.'

Olivier sat down at Jeanne's feet and leant his head back between her knees. She was wearing black woollen tights and a green skirt. He tore off the end of one foot of her tights with his teeth and, using his fingers, widened the hole to let her toes out.

'Fucking tights and socks, I can't stand all these extra layers of skin.'

'We won't wear them on the island.'

'No, they'll be banned. Anyone with socks on will have his legs chopped off.'

*Fragments of pink rubber were dangling from the trees all around. He didn't know what had burst but he knew it was his fault. The sun's reddish rays set a brass band playing inside his head. The sand was scorching and soft, up to his ankles as he tried to run away. It was hard going; the beach was sloped, as was the horizon. His calves hardened like marble as he went. The sweat dripping into his eyes blurred the yellow and blue. Everything was turning green and from green to violet, purple, burning bright …*

Jeanne's tights were rolled down to the middle of her thighs. A tuft of hair was just visible between her buttocks. A trickle of sperm ran from one to the other. The underside of the coffee table looked like the ceiling of a cottage for dwarves. Olivier poked his head out, leaning on his elbows. The coir rug had left patterns on his knees. His swollen penis rested against his left thigh. He could have drunk the ocean and all its fish. The warm, flat dregs of champagne barely lifted his tongue off his palate. He could feel something crawling along his leg, then over his stomach, up his back, neck, cheeks … It was ants, hundreds of microscopic ants.

'Filthy pieces of shit!'

He leapt up, knocking over the table and the champagne glasses on top of it. The trousers around his ankles prevented him from running. No matter how he slapped and scratched himself, more kept coming, columns of ants taking over his body. Jeanne propped herself up on one elbow.

'What are you doing? What's the matter?'

'Stand up, for God's sake! There are ants everywhere! Get up!'

Olivier hurried into the bathroom, tore off his clothes and turned the shower on, not caring whether the water was hot or cold. The insects slid off his skin by the dozen and swirled down the plughole. When he had got rid of them all, Olivier turned off the water and rubbed himself with his towel until he drew blood. Jeanne was leaning on the sink watching him.

'Filthy disgusting pieces of shit! Did you see? We need to buy a spray or something … Can you check my back, make sure they're all gone.'

'You're fine, there's not one left.'

'Aren't there any on you?'

'No.'

'That's weird … You saw them though, didn't you? You did see?'

'Yes, but they're gone now.'

'We should still give it a vacuum.'

'I'll do it. You get yourself dressed.'

'Have a good look all over because they're tiny; they'll end up getting in through the pores of your skin and poisoning your blood. I should know.'

'Jeanne, there's nothing left to drink. You don't fancy going down to the old lady, do you?'

So Jeanne went down and bought any old thing, since they were on bottle number forty-something. Twice, sometimes three times a day, for the last week. Olivier no longer wanted to go out, no longer could. She felt as if she was living with two different Oliviers: the one who studied the map of Mauritius in the atlas with her, describing in detail the smells of Goodlands market, the colour of the parrotfish on the boats at Grand Gaube, the quality of the shade around Trou-aux-Biches, and another who kept half an eye trained on the alcohol stocks, constantly looked for ants and made himself bleed scratching himself, who fell asleep mid-sentence and snored with his mouth wide open. It was impossible to predict at what point he would switch from one to the other. They hadn't made love since the ant invasion. When he was calm, he stroked her hair, kissed the sides of her head, lightly brushed her lips, no more, like a shy child. The rest of the time, he was too pissed to manage anything. He would get annoyed, turning his back to her and masturbating so hard he put his shoulder out, but to no avail. The truth was she couldn't care less; the caresses and butterfly kisses were enough for her. Olivier was what he was, but he was here, and that was all she asked for. Rodolphe had gone to join her father, mother and two brothers in the family vault. A few neighbours and local people intrigued by the unusual manner of his death had come to see him off. Sitting in the front row was the ubiquitous Madeleine.

'Well, you know, he might be better off up there! He wasn't

happy here with us. It has to be said, being in the dark the whole time … well, it would send me mad! Some get used to it, others never do. Oh, I meant to ask, is he still there?'

'Who?'

'The other one, your neighbour opposite, your friend whose mother died.'

'I think so.'

'It's odd because I never see him any more. I've knocked on his door a few times but he never answers. He drinks a lot, you know. You don't think he might have done something stupid too? Ought we perhaps to tell someone?'

'That would be a bit much for one floor, Madame Lasson. I saw him going out yesterday. He must be busy sorting out his mother's affairs.'

'Oh right. That's us oldies for you, worrying about nothing. Actually, if you see him again, would you tell him I need to speak to him. His poor mother promised to pass on a couple of things should anything happen to her. Oh, nothing of much worth, it's more sentimental than anything.'

'I'll tell him.'


Olivier couldn't give a shit; the stupid old bitch could take whatever she wanted, as long as he didn't have to see her. He couldn't face dealing with it all anyway. All he wanted was to drink and sleep between these four walls, with the curtains hermetically sealed. There was no day or night. New Year's Eve came and went unnoticed despite the shouting and popping of corks. Clinging to one another, they stopped up the hourglass; time had come to a standstill above their heads. The walls of the bedroom were papered with gaudy images of palm-fringed beaches, turquoise water and brightly coloured flowers from the brochures Jeanne picked up in travel agents' on her rare trips out of the flat. Olivier gave an ever more frenzied commentary on them, telling the same anecdote ten times, diving onto the bed, swimming between the sheets until he fell back, pointing at the wall and delivering one last piece of advice.

'Past the coral reef, there are sharks. You must never go there, ever!'

Jeanne never tired of listening to him, nibbling on dried fruit or biscuits. That was all they fed themselves on now. She watched him sleep, lying diagonally across the unmade bed, so pale, his hair stuck to his brow, like a sailor washed up on the shore after a shipwreck. He was the master of the island, this island that did not exist on any map but which he brought into being every day, just for her. Only he knew the way. No one else had ever taken her so far, in all her life. There was as much difference between him and the best of the rest as between an illusionist and a magician. The first knew how to manipulate, the second how to create, to give himself entirely at the risk of reducing himself to ashes. That's why it was up to her to mark out the territory, to ensure nothing could stall their progress.

The holidays were nearing their end. The school had granted her request for indefinite leave without question. The circumstances of her brother's death could not be argued with. She had also convinced Olivier to send a note to his wife to the effect that he had taken his mother's death worse than he had first thought and was going to spend some time with friends in the country, step back a bit. And of course, she mustn't worry.

None of this solved anything, it just bought them some time, but that was all they needed, for time to stand still.

Besides the bedroom and bathroom, they had stopped using the rest of the flat, which was becoming cloaked in dust. Olivier would no longer set foot in it, because of the ants. Some of them still managed to sneak into the bedroom, but the majority of the colony were gathered in there, under the coffee table. In any case, they didn't know what to do with all the space.

They didn't need it. Sometimes even the bedroom felt too big. When that happened, they would retreat to the bed and allow it to drift until the walls disappeared completely. Bottles, biscuit wrappers, dried-fruit packets and other detritus gathered around the edges of the room, softening the corners of the walls. The jumbled laundry towered high in the bathroom, so they lived in their dressing gowns. Jeanne had set aside one outfit for her excursions, which she referred to as her wetsuit. This was exactly how it felt going out onto the street, a sea bed crisscrossed by shoals of passers-by, or deserted, totally still but for the rippling of the trees. Everything seemed to move incredibly slowly, every sound appeared muffled. It wasn't unpleasant, it was just another world, and she was only passing through. She sometimes told Olivier about it when she got home.

'Everyone looks sad and gloomy. They're taking the lights down. It's the first week of the sales, all the bedding's reduced.'

He went 'Ah', poking his nose into the carrier bags she had brought back with her, taking out a bottle and setting sail for Pamplemousses Botanical Gardens. Beyond what could be eaten or drunk, everything that came from outside was akin to pollution. He had unplugged the phone and nailed down the curtains so no light or sound could get in. The stench of dustbins, tobacco and ant-killer, which he used in abundance, made the atmosphere almost solid. They didn't mind it. It was their smell, the scent of their island.

Madeleine had come knocking again two days after Rodolphe's funeral. Jeanne fobbed her off by telling her Olivier had gone but had left her his keys, and Madeleine was welcome to take anything she liked.

'Anything! … Say what you like, but he's a bit of an oddball that one. Off he goes without a word of goodbye … Well, I'm not complaining; in any case it's what his poor mother wanted.

You wouldn't know anyone who could help me get the fridge down, would you?'

Since then, they hadn't seen anybody. Soon they would be forgotten completely, lost at sea without a trace. There was no need to make plans, they just lay back and let the current take them.

A few had managed to get into his anus and start munching on him from the inside. Classic ant tactic. He had been shitting blood for several days. The only way to treat it was to knock back a large glass of Ricard on an empty stomach and spew it straight up again. Sucked into the digestive maelstrom, the bastards came out through his mouth and disappeared into the toilet bowl. Afterwards, he took a shower and scrubbed himself with an exfoliating glove.

He was drying his hair when Jeanne stuck her head round the door.

'I'm off. I'm going all the way to Monoprix; we're out of everything.'

'Don't forget the Raid, the last can's almost empty. I threw up five of them this morning.'

'I won't. See you later.'

He didn't like it when she went out. She always brought a bit of the outside in with her in the folds of her clothes and her hair, and it reawakened bad thoughts. Memories from his life before rose back up to the surface and he no longer knew which world he belonged to. He felt trapped, his path peppered with mines whichever way he turned. He didn't dare make the slightest move, and felt himself tumbling into a narrowing crater. He began to doubt everything, even Jeanne. Of course someone had to do the shopping, but was that all she was doing? What if Rodolphe wasn't dead after all? What if Madeleine and Odile and the rest of their petty little world had joined forces to set the ants on him? Why would they? There were any number of reasons, but it all came down to the same thing: to blame him for all their crimes. Deep down, everyone had something to feel bad about, so just think: an alcoholic who can't remember anything, how's that for a scapegoat?

He pulled a bottle of rum out from under the bed and filled the tooth glass. It was all becoming clear, perfectly logical. Logic was his lifeline: it came with the first drink, drawing all the inconsistencies of his existence together in one reassuringly balanced mosaic. While operating in the realm of logic, he displayed Machiavellian wile. He found reasons for everything and made acrobatic connections between the most contradictory elements of his situation until he had formed a convoluted web of certainty which echoed the complex patterns of his mother's doilies. He understood everything, not just about his own life; he was party to the secrets of the entire universe: the workings of the planets, gas engines, squaring the circle, the fluctuations of the stock market, the best way to make mayonnaise, everything. It all held together, it all came from him. And then … one of Jeanne's hairs on a comb was enough to bring the monumental structure crashing down in an instant.

'What the hell am I going on about? I haven't just got ants in the arse, they're getting into my brain too! Forgive me, Jeanne! You shouldn't leave me on my own …'

In a split second, he went from the role of victim of a universal conspiracy to that of the most abject of traitors. The alcohol he was absorbing was immediately shed again as hot tears. He chucked the bottle across the bedroom and bolted into the bathroom.

'Forgive me, Jeanne, forgive me … You'll see, everything's going to change. I'm going to stop drinking, we'll get the hell out of here and go to a nice clean island. I'll shave, get dressed ...'

His reflection in the mirror of the bathroom cabinet terrified him. Pale, almost green skin with a straggly beard and unkempt hair, the whites of his eyes pastis-yellow and bloodshot. With his hands shaking uncontrollably, he grabbed the shaving foam and razor.

He did his hair as if preparing for the school photo, slicked over to one side. His face was red raw with cuts all over his skin. The 'after' picture was not much of an improvement on the 'before'. The sides of the sink looked like the dregs of a raspberry sundae, froth and blood. Jeanne's perfume, which he slapped all over himself, set fire to his cheeks. Then he put on the freshest clothes he could find and sat on the edge of the bed, stunned at the amount of energy he had just expended. Why wasn't Jeanne home? She should have been there to witness his metamorphosis. He needed to see her, right now this instant. Rodolphe's videos! There were dozens of tapes of Jeanne.

Olivier sprayed an entire can of Raid under the coffee table before settling down in front of the VCR. He chose a tape at random and inserted it into the machine. On the screen, he saw a glass salad bowl in pieces on the kitchen floor accompanied by the sound of swearing and Rodolphe laughing: 'Newsflash!' Afterwards, the camera swung in figures of eight following the broom as it swept the shards of glass into a dustpan. The only bit of Jeanne on show was her yellow rubber-gloved hands. In the background, water was running.

She must have been in the middle of doing the washing-up. The dustpan was emptied into the bin and the lens abruptly moved up to frame Jeanne's face with her tongue sticking out. Her hair was shorter, her cheeks more rounded. Then she turned her back to the camera and it cut to another sequence. Jeanne reading, Jeanne smoking, Jeanne sewing a button back on, Jeanne marking homework, Jeanne angry, Jeanne smiling, in winter, in summer, by night, by day, in the lounge, on a path in the park. And often Jeanne sleeping, a book lying open in her hand, lips parted, a strand of hair falling over her eyes.

Tape after tape, Jeanne's life was piling up at Olivier's feet. Every so often he stopped on a frame and if he could place it to a particular date or time of year, he tried to remember what he had been doing at the same time. All the years he had spent without her, now he could see them through the eyes of a blind man. It was Rodolphe's memories scrolling in front of him and yet he was sure he would have filmed exactly the same things.

Olivier ejected the tape that had just ended and replaced it with another. This must be more recent; he recognised the clothes Jeanne was wearing. She was watching television. She seemed annoyed.

'Rodolphe, will you stop that?'

'What's the matter, don't want anyone to see you sulking?'

'I'm not sulking. You're annoying me with the camcorder. Stop it, please.'

Next there was a close-up of a cheese rind and a crust of bread on a plate. When he heard the key in the lock, Olivier put the TV on mute and went to the front door. He felt the need to hold her tightly in his arms.

Jeanne met Inspector Luneau just outside the building. He had crossed from the opposite pavement.

'Hello, I was in the area so I thought I'd drop by. I tried to call you but I couldn't get through. Is it OK if I come up for a minute? We've got some new information on the man found in the woods. It won't take long.'

'Um ... yes.'

'Allow me.'

Luneau took the shopping bags out of her hands and stepped back to let her go ahead. As she climbed the stairs, Jeanne felt a growing sense of dread, like that feeling when you're sure you have forgotten something, but you don't know what. However, the inspector had given no cause for alarm; he didn't seem to have come bearing bad news. Once he reached the landing, Luneau put the bags down, gasping for breath.

'Blimey, this must be your monthly shop!'

Jeanne's little laugh was cut dead when she opened the door and came face to face with Olivier standing in the doorway as stiff as a statue, arms outstretched, a fixed smile on his face, hair neatly combed as if on his way to first communion, skin ripped to pieces as if he had just fought off a wild cat. He looked like a waxwork. Jeanne had to collect herself before making the introductions.

'Inspector Luneau, this is my friend Olivier Verdier.'

Olivier gave his clammy hand to the police officer and moved aside to let him pass. Jeanne gave him a look of reassurance. Olivier picked up the shopping and took it into the kitchen while Jeanne and Luneau sat down in the living room. Soundless images were dancing about on the TV screen. Jeanne got up to turn it off, but the inspector stopped her.

'Leave it on, it doesn't bother me. The kids have it on twenty-four hours a day at home, and that's with the sound on! Anyway, do you know this man?'

The photo he was holding up to her was of an ageless man with thinning brown hair and a moustache.

'No, never seen him. He looks like any other man in the street.'

'It's funny you should say that. We picked him up in Viroflay in possession of documents belonging to the man found strangled in Fausses-Reposes. He admits finding the body on the morning of the 24th and taking the money and ID, but surprise surprise, he denies having killed him. He's homeless, a total alcoholic. He keeps changing his story. Luc Gaignon – doesn't ring any bells?'

'None. So where does this leave my brother?'

'To tell you the truth, we're finding it hard to make sense of what he did. The fact he was the only suspect might explain it at a push, even if the idea of a blind person – albeit a very independent one – having dragged a fit young man several kilometres into the forest in the middle of the night, strangled him and cheerfully made his way home again always seemed pretty far-fetched.'

'It does seem unlikely, I have to say.'

'Unless he had someone with him, like Gaignon. Only Gaignon says he doesn't know any blind people.'

'I ... I don't know what to say.'

'Don't worry about it. I think as far as you're concerned, we're just about done. We got in touch with the psychiatrist who was looking after your brother and he confirmed what you said. Who knows what was going through his mind when he jumped ... Could I possibly trouble you for a glass of water? I'm taking tablets for a cold and they really dry my mouth out.'

'Of course, just a second.'

Jeanne left the living room. Luneau automatically turned towards the screen. A family scene – he took home videos too – looked like Christmas Eve dinner. He recognised the gentleman he had passed in the hallway, only more cleanly shaven, Mademoiselle Mangin and …

'Jesus Christ!'

The guy from the woods, Roland Whatsisname, alive and well and stuffing his face.

The jug of water struck him right on the temple. Jeanne had flung it with all her might. The inspector's body brought the chair down with it. Olivier emerged from the kitchen, can of Raid in hand.

'What's going on?'

'Will you turn that off, please?'

Roland was in close-up, pulling faces and waving a chicken thigh at the camera.

Olivier tried in vain to think of the right thing to say in the circumstances: 'I'm sorry, I didn't mean to, I apologise …' He made do with repeating 'SHIT' while shaking his head at the grey screen. As for Jeanne, she had to hand it to her brother. He was still managing to ruin their lives from beyond the grave. One last act, just as everything was settling down. Neither of them spared a thought for Luneau until he began groaning and wiggling his fingers.

'He's not dead?'

'He's moving …'

The little bit of life left in the inspector's body made it even more of an encumbrance. Just as with little Luc, there was no need to discuss it first. Both of their hands instinctively reached for one of the sofa cushions. Olivier straddled Luneau's chest, holding his arms down with his knees, while Jeanne placed the cushion over his face. A split second before it was covered up, Olivier thought he saw on it the same expression of surprise as he had seen on little Luc's. Facing each other on all fours, they were like two wild beasts bringing down their prey. Pressing their fingernails into the pliable fabric, they kept their eyes locked, drawing energy from one another to overcome Luneau's jerking. As insignificant as he was, the cop was displaying a remarkable will to live. Olivier was obliged to lie almost flat on top of him in order to hold his legs down. It was like a grotesque coupling, a tragic rodeo ride. And then nothing, just an echo of Luneau fading into the silence of the living room.

'Do you think we can stop?'

'A bit longer. He might be pretending.'

'Yes … What are we going to do with him?'

'I don't know. Across the hall, in your mother's place?'

'Yes, for now … but then what?'

'I don't know, Olivier! Sometimes you just have to do things without wasting time thinking about it.'

'Let's dump him across the hall then.'

'I think we're good to go.'

They slowly lifted the cushion, ready to pounce at the slightest flutter of the lashes. But there was nothing left to fear from the inspector.

'I think he looks a bit confused, don't you? Frowning, the lower lip sticking out slightly …'

'Well, it must have come as a bit of a shock, after all. Check he hasn't left anything lying around on the table. Let's carry him over there straight away.'

They carted Luneau from one home to the other with the breezy efficiency of two old hands. Once the armchair had been put right in the lounge, they could have sworn to anybody that no policeman had ever set foot in there. Olivier had got it into his head to knock up an exotic cocktail. Jeanne followed him into the kitchen. With her fingertip, she traced figures of eight on the tablecloth while he mixed very unequal proportions of rum and passion fruit.

'OK, so his colleagues rock up. I'll be the cop and you answer. Mademoiselle Mangin, did you see Inspector Plumeau …'

'Luneau!'

'Sorry, Luneau, yesterday?'

'No, I didn't.'

'And yet he was supposed to visit you and no one has seen him since.'

'I don't know what else I can tell you. I didn't see him.'

'And yet his car is parked just around the corner from your apartment.'

'Huh, how do you know?'

'I don't, but it probably is. Do you have any objection to us searching your apartment?'

'None at all.'

Olivier tested his concoction and added the juice of a lemon and a little more alcohol.

'Not bad … Nothing here, boss! … They'll ask you to remain at their disposal, of course. We'll buy ourselves a day, maybe two … Do you want to try it?'

'No, thanks. And then?'

'You should, it'll buck you up. And then … we have to get to the island before they eat us!'

In spite of the face covered in shaving cuts, Olivier looked more like a child who had just played a good trick than a murderer.

'Leave, you mean?'

'We left ages ago. We're almost there now.'

'Yes, but we need to leave the house, get in the car, cross the border, go quickly, before the police …'

'It sounds like you're describing the story of a bad movie. The police? What police? Get over it, Jeanne, you're losing the plot.'

Olivier knelt down in front of her and took hold of her hands. He was smiling at her.

'Are you afraid?'

'Yes. I am now. They're going to come, Olivier. Luneau …'

'What about Luneau? Who is Luneau? There is no Luneau, not any more! There never was!'

He stood up suddenly, his face changed, pale, tense, his right eyelid twitching. He began furiously scratching his forearms, muttering between gritted teeth: 'Bastards … Bastards!' He lunged for his cocktail and downed the whole glass in one. Then he took his head in his hands, his chin dropped and his whole body slumped to the ground, as if a hand holding him by the neck had suddenly released its grasp.

'You've stopped believing, Jeanne. You're abandoning me.'

'I'm not, my love, I'm just trying to find a solution. I think I remember Luneau saying he wasn't on an official visit. "I happened to be in the area," is what he said. We can be long gone by the time they make the connection. We can do it, my love; it's possible!'

Olivier's head was resting on Jeanne's shoulder. A tear was following the contours of his nose. He could feel it running down, seeking the path to the corner of his mouth. Poor Jeanne. They had managed to infect her. She was thinking like them, crime, police, prison, escape … They were no longer on the same wavelength. The island was within touching distance and she could no longer see it. He would have to man the helm alone. It would be difficult, but he felt up to the task.

'OK?'

'Yes.'

'Then I'll throw a few things into a bag and we'll get going.'

'OK then.'

Jeanne disappeared into the bedroom. Olivier got up, took the bunch of keys from Jeanne's bag and the spare set from the dresser and double-locked all the locks on the door. Afterwards he flushed both sets down the toilet. Jeanne had caused them to take on water, but it was OK, he had plugged the leak.

Now it was all watertight again. In spite of everything, there was air getting in under the blasted door and through the kitchen window too; he had felt it earlier. He went off in search of cloths to stick into the cracks. Nothing more must flow in or out.

'What are you doing?'

Olivier was nailing a bedcover over the kitchen window.

'Good timing. Could you take the right-hand corner please?'

'But … Olivier, I've almost finished packing. We're leaving!'

'Can you help me please, there's air getting in. Can't you feel it?'

'Who cares! Leave all that and come with me.'

Olivier let the hammer dangle in his hand and sighed deeply.

'Jeanne, my little Jeanne. You were perfect up until now, but you're cracking in the last phase of the journey. It's OK, I understand. But now you need to trust me and let me get on with what needs to be done. There you go, you take the right-hand corner of this cover and hold it up while I do the left, OK?'

He spoke calmly, pronouncing each word clearly and patiently like an adult addressing a child. Jeanne took the cover and pressed it up against the window. Olivier was hammering his nails in with care. She was sure he must be humming in his head, like he did when building tree houses. She on the ground, he up in the trees. She didn't know how to get him down any more. When his work was done, he jumped down from the sink on which he was perched and ran his hand along each side of the window.

'Perfect! Not a whisper of a breeze.'

'Good. So can we go now then?'

'What about the other windows? And the gap under the door? We're a long way from being finished, sweetheart!'

'Olivier, listen to me. We still have a chance …'

'Of course we do! What's the matter? You seem tense.'

'Olivier, we take our bags, go downstairs, get in the car, and a few hours from now we'll be far away—'

'Far away? What do you know about far away? We're far away right where we are. You should stop listening to the sirens, they give bad advice. You're starting to be afraid of your own fear. You mustn't – I'm here, I know the way. Leave it to me. Come with me.'

Olivier took her by the wrist and started leading her towards the bedroom. His hand was hot and sticky. As they passed the front door, Jeanne broke free and made a grab for the handle, but it would not open.

'Jeanne, don't be stupid.'

'Where are the keys?'

'They've gone. We're free now – do you understand? Free! There's nothing to open or lock up any more.'

She let him carry her into the bedroom and tie her to the bed frame.

There were cracks and crannies all over the place. No sooner had he finished filling one than he spotted another, in a corner or along a skirting board. It was a Herculean task, but he did not let himself lose heart. On the other side of the wall, he could hear the outside rumbling, its waves swelling, ready to break. It would have been handy to have Jeanne's help, but she could no longer be relied upon. She had given up. Their survival depended on him alone. He finished stuffing a sock between two floorboards and stood up. He was dripping with sweat and his head was spinning. He made one last inspection of the flat, paying particular attention to the weak spots such as windows and doors, and returned to the bedroom, satisfied.

'It's all looking good, sweetheart. It's just a quick fix, but it'll hold until we reach the coast. Now we just have to go with the flow.'

They were lying against one another, calm and relaxed. The bed seemed to sway slightly, rocking them gently.

'Olivier?'

'Yes?'

'I just wanted to tell you … it was me who killed Roland.'

'Oh.'

'After you both left, I got up. I met Rodolphe on his way to bed. He told me you were leaving in the morning. I went over to your flat. You were asleep. I tried to wake you up, but you were out for the count. I heard Roland being sick in the bathroom. I picked up your tie. I wanted you to stay.'

'You did the right thing. I probably would have left, and then I'd never have seen the island again. Rodolphe guessed, didn't he?'

'Yes.'

'I can untie you now ...'

'No, I'd rather you didn't. I can still hear the sirens, it's like flushes of fever and then it passes, and I trust you.'

'I'm hungry, aren't you?'

'No.'

'Come on, you have to eat! I'll make us something.'

Jeanne was staring up at the middle of the ceiling, where a wire was dangling from a wreath-shaped ceiling rose. It was her North Star. Olivier was right, it was important to stay on course. The bubble was sealed, no one could see in any more. While they were stifling little Luc's cries in the cabin, a group of ramblers had passed within a metre of them and hadn't seen or suspected a thing. To them, Jeanne and Olivier had never existed.

'*Non, non, ma fille, tu n'iras pas danser ...*' That's what they were singing. '*Mets ta robe blanche et ta ceinture dorée ...*'

Jeanne was humming the tune. The song did her good, like a glass of cold water at the end of a long walk.

Olivier felt like having a proper meal. For the first time in several days, he had the urge to eat something hot. Noodles. Yes, noodles and ham, and sardines for starters and tinned fruit for dessert. He juggled the tins and packets, unsure where to start. It was quite an undertaking because he was trying to think of everything all at once and he only had two arms. The packaging was hard to rip off, he couldn't find the tin opener and all the plates were dirty. He was obliged to finish the bottle of rum to calm his culinary fervour. The thing was, there was no messing around any more, everything rested on his shoulders, he had to keep an eye on everything. It was a big responsibility! He had just put a pan of water on the hob and turned on the gas when he felt something slip between his feet. It had jumped out of the dustbin and disappeared through a hole in the corner of the room the size of a five-franc piece. Olivier blew out the match he had been about to use to light the gas.

'Shit! A rat.'

Yes, it was a rat, and not a mouse! It was enormous. It was just about possible to cope with ants, but rats were another story. It was absolutely imperative to block up that hole. But not with bits of cloth or wood; those creatures could gnaw through anything. It took him a while to nail a jam lid over the opening, but it was worth the effort. He felt slightly faint when he tried to stand up again. The atmosphere was heavy, leaden, as if a storm was on its way. His muscles went floppy like marshmallow at the slightest move. There was a persistent whistling sound in his head. Sitting on the floor with his arms between his legs, he saw the tiles undulating as his stomach heaved. Food, that was what he had come in here for ... He had to take food back for Jeanne ... That was why he was feeling so weak. They needed to build their strength in order to brave the rising tempest. He managed to grab a packet of biscuits and drag himself into the hallway, where he lay down on his back. He seemed to breathe a little more easily.

Jeanne had heard a series of loud knocks. Her whole being had closed up like a fist. She had arched up off the bed and tugged on her binds. She didn't want ... what exactly? She wasn't sure, but she didn't want it. She refused it all out of hand. She would have liked to scream NO in capital letters, but the air got stuck in her throat like coal dust. The ceiling was coming down, weighing on her chest …

'Jeanne, can you see it? … Over there … There are still clouds around the peaks, but it's sunny on the beach. Tell me you can see it?'

Olivier's hand on her breast was warm and soothing.

'Yes, I can see it … I'm tired. It's been such a long, long time …'

'It's over now. It's over …'

They came smoothly alongside as the biscuits scattered on the floor.

'Well, a smell like that! … I was taking my bin out. I didn't think twice, I just called the fire brigade.'

'Excuse me a minute, Madeleine … How many croissants was it?'

Madeleine moved aside to let the woman serve her customer.

'Twelve francs fifty, thank you … And then what?'

'And then they came straight away. Say what you like, but the fire brigade … Anyway, they come up, knock on the door, no reply. It smelt of gas so, you know … They knock the door down and … I didn't see the rest, of course, they wouldn't let me in, but I heard them. Well, turns out they'd sealed the whole place up, all the doors and windows. Mademoiselle Mangin, well, she was tied to the bed, so I heard, TIED UP! Can you imagine?'

'A *baguette à l'ancienne*? … That'll be eight francs sixty, thank you. Tied up! I don't believe it!'

'I'm telling you, it's true! Wait, that's not all! I saw them bringing out the stretchers and who should I see lying on one of them but the neighbour! Rather, the neighbour's son. You remember poor Madame Verdier, who died just before Christmas?'

'Yes, the one you used to take care of.'

'That's right. I go, "He's still here!" because Mademoiselle Mangin had told me he'd left. "Do you know him?" says a big fellow who tells me he's with the police. I reply, "Do I ever" and "He lives across the hall". So they break his door down and what do you think they find inside? I'll give you three guesses.'

'We've run out of rye bread, Madame. Would you like wholemeal instead? ... Well, what was it?'

'The body of a man, and not just anyone. A police officer!'

'No!'

'Yes!'

'Nine francs eighty, thanks. What a story!'

'It's knocked me sideways. You don't know who you're living next door to these days.'

'No, quite ... You poor thing ... Will it be the usual *bâtard* then?'

'The usual.'